SECRET DIARY SERIES

LEE SWIFT

KRIS COOK

MISTY'S SPANKING DIARY

Jan 1st

Here's my first entry.
What to say?
This is much harder than I thought. I haven't written in one of
these since I was thirteen when I had a crush on my eighth grade
science teacher, Mr. Blackwell. That seems a hundred years ago, but
it's only been twelve, almost half my life.

Mmm.

Often times my thoughts get all jumbled up. I remember the last
time I had to give a speech in a class. What a mess! Thankfully, I rarely
have to speak publicly. It's a bit of a phobia with me. I took out a butt
load of student loans to avoid the road many grad students take – the
dreaded prof's aide.

God, I sound boring.

Keeping a diary seemed like such a good idea last night when I
bought this. Now, I'm not so sure. Isn't keeping a journal of your
thoughts more of an adolescent activity than that of a college grad
working on her master's in sociology? Mostly true. But I need a
distraction from all the dead-end research of my fucking thesis.

"Fucking?" LOL!

Why the hell did I choose the topic: "Principals and Practices of

Participants of Bondage and Discipline, 'Sadomasochism' or Dominance and Submission (BDSM)?" One reason was to impress my adviser, the head of the department, Dr. Emily Vickers. What to say about Dr. Vickers? The day I gave the title of my thesis to the emotionless iceberg, her lips actually curled up just a bit. It didn't shock her like I'd wanted. I have to admit I kind of wanted to watch the woman faint. Instead I'd felt something like satisfaction roll over her. Weird, but it was her first positive feedback about my work. I would've liked a little more from her, but the nonverbal reaction would have to suffice. Still, I decided to count that small smile as a victory.

Now, four months later with no real data to speak of, I think I may have painted myself into a corner.

I chose to write about sex. Smart, Mia. Really smart. I haven't had that much experience with sex, but that's not to say I'm totally naive about it.

I've had four boyfriends. The first one in ninth grade turned out to be gay. We're still friends. The next two, not so much. The last one was really sweet, and I get a birthday card from him every year.

My first straight boyfriend was a virgin just like I was at the time. We fumbled our way through that first night together. He came. I didn't. In fact, I never did reach orgasm the four more times we had sex. It was fun, though, and his kissing did improve over the year we were together. Unfortunately, his dad got transferred to Japan, and I never saw him again.

I met my next boyfriend the first week of my freshman year in college. He instantly came off as honest and sweet. Turned out that the prick was a liar and cheater. During the seven months we were together, he was with three other women. I did climax with him a few times, but my vibrator worked so much better to pleasure me than his dick ever did.

That's not entirely true.

There was one time when he introduced me to spanking. I was soaked and had my one and only multiple-orgasm. He awoke something inside me that has lingered under my buttoned-up surface ever since. He'd pulled out a paddle that was flat and round. It had looked a little like an oversized version of a ping-pong paddle and had me mesmerized the instant I saw it. I'd just known that it would do something for me. Maybe that was why I'd bared my ass and knelt on all fours. Not for him in particular, but for that paddle and where I thought it might take me. Fuck, that experience was fantastic, and if I'd not found out what a motherfucker he was, I might've stayed with him longer just to feel his paddle on my ass every night.

My last boyfriend was really nice. But everything with him was so vanilla, including sex. There was quite a bit of it over the fourteen months we were together, but I never reached orgasm. God, I tried. It may sound crazy, but he was too sweet. I got flowers once a month, and he always let me pick which restaurant to go to. It was exhausting. Whenever I offered to help him with errands or whatever, he would tell me he had it covered. He didn't understand why I broke it off with him, but I had to.

If I'm honest with myself, the real reason I chose BDSM as the topic for my thesis was to satisfy my own curiosity. You see, thinking about my ex-boyfriend spanking me gets me wet and dizzy. Even now, just writing about it is giving me tingles.

Shall I be totally honest? Why not? This is never going to be read by anyone.

The truth is that when I masturbate, I imagine getting spanked by a tall, muscular man. Sometimes this fantasy man is Mr. Blackwell, the aforementioned authoritative science teacher with dark hair and a voice like gravel mixed with honey. Other times he's uniformed and so very serious. There are at least a dozen more mini-movies I run through my mind to get off. My favorite is the man who climbs in through the window while I'm sleeping. That last one never fails to send me to the moon.

Sick, sure. I'm probably a cautionary *Lifetime* movie waiting to happen, but I'm being brutally honest here.

That's enough about my illicit fantasies. See what I mean about my mind wandering? Let me get back to where I'm at with my thesis.

Things haven't turned out quite the way I thought they would for my paper. I must get real data from actual people if I have any chance of getting my thesis to a state that will earn me my master's degree. I've tried to get interviews with people practicing BDSM. Trouble is that if you're an outsider, they don't want to talk to you. I'm what they affectionately call a tourist. Except without the affection. I even went to several exclusive clubs—the key word being "exclusive." No luck. I couldn't get past the front door.

I've shared my difficulties with Dr. Vickers, who couldn't seem more disinterested if she tried. Her lackluster answer was to recommend I attend a lecture tomorrow night she's hosting. Tomorrow night! Classes don't start back up until Monday, January 12th. The woman hates me. With her as my adviser, I'm definitely on my own, that's for sure. A dull lecture is the last thing I need to finish my paper. I have half a mind to blow the boring lecture off. Maybe I'm not as much of a masochist as I thought, but she's damn straight a sadist.

Knowing that it's just you and me, diary, gives me courage to state my true feelings. For example: Dr. Vickers is a coldhearted bitch!

That felt so freeing. Expressing my intimate feelings here is going to be nice.

I guess I'll go to the lecture just to keep Dr. Vickers off my back.

I think I'm going to enjoy this journaling.

That's all for tonight.

Jan 2nd

❧❀❧

Oh boy, diary.

God, I'm in my bed and still reeling from what just happened to me at the BDSM club.

Wait. Let me backtrack and get my thoughts in order, though the way I'm feeling, that might be hard to do. I can't believe I actually jumped into this whole thing with my ass in the air—and for someone I just met.

Oh, God! I've never experienced anything like it.

Damn. His hand on my ass had me reeling from a million sensations.

I can't do this right now.

I'll be back.

∿

Okay. Better. Thank you Dr. Feel Good. Oh, that's what I named my vibrator.

Let me get back to the events of this amazing night.

It all started when I arrived at the lecture Dr. Vickers had told me to attend. I had thought about blowing it off. I'm so glad that I didn't.

I went to the lecture in the hopes of garnering an interview or at least some takeaways for my master's thesis, but what I received was much more than I could've ever expected.

There were only fifteen people in attendance. Dr. Vickers passed around a sign-in sheet for the undergrads. Apparently, she was giving them some extra credit for attending. When my nemesis saw me enter, she pointed to the chair in the center of the front row, indicating that was where she expected me to sit. And though it pissed me off, I still complied. I don't know what it is about me that I respond so easily to authority, even when I despise the person. A firm voice and a dismissive wave of a hand and I find myself unable to resist.

The rest of the attendees sat behind me from the third row to the last row. I sat alone with my hands in my lap like a little schoolgirl. Awkward. Sums up my life.

Then *he* walked in.

The speaker instantly had my heart pounding in my chest and my breath hitching in my lungs. He overflowed with confidence and power with each step, like a gladiator coming on the field to defeat anyone foolish enough to challenge him. In his early thirties, the man's coal black hair was cut razor short, and his face, though not Hollywood handsome, had a ruggedness that made me squirm in the metal chair. His jaw was square, and he sported a five o'clock shadow. His eyes were so piercing blue I found myself unable to look away. In fact, every woman in the place was near drooling over his six-foot-five muscled frame. The speaker's arrival instantly silenced the chatter among the other males in the room. Their combined testosterone would barely fill a thimble compared to his.

Dr. Vickers stepped up to the lectern and pounded on it with her fist. "Quiet students."

Since no one was talking, I found her command odd. Oh, well. I knew I would never figure her out.

"Welcome. Tonight continues our series on Human Sexuality in the Modern Age. This is our fifth lecture. Our guest speaker is the owner of The Cell, located downtown, one of the most notable BDSM clubs in the country. He's won several awards for his work with special effects. He's written several bestselling books about the lifestyle including *The Path of Dominance and Submission*; *The Master's Rules*; and *The Guide to Creating Your Home Dungeon*. He also hosts a weekly Q & A podcast for people deep in the life, just beginning, or only curious called "The Spanking Bench."

I gasped aloud the instant Dr. Vickers mentioned the name of the speaker's Internet show, but thankfully, no one seemed to notice.

"Students, welcome our guest, Master Lex Brogan."

Clapping, I felt my temperature go up several degrees as his searing blue eyes seemed to fix on me.

"Thank you, Dr. Vickers for inviting me. Instead of giving a boring speech from a stale outline, I'm going to have you ask me questions, and I will answer them. Got it?"

"Yes, thank you," I said, as if he and I were the only ones in the room.

"Good." He paused. In a deep, commanding tone that startled me, he said, "Front Row, you go first."

"Me?" I pointed to the center of my chest.

"Is there anyone else on the front row?"

"No." My mouth was suddenly dry, and my mind turned to mush. "Umm. I am...working on...it's a paper. I mean...I have this paper that I have to finish. It's called 'Principals and Practices of Participants of Bondage and Discipline, "Sadomasochism" or Dominance and Submission' and it's required to earn my master's." Every word I uttered made me sound more and more idiotic. Why did my mind always spin with a million conflicting thoughts, paralyzing me to act or to even speak coherently?

"I'm sure there's a question in there somewhere."

I shook my head. "Mr. Brogan—"

"It's 'Master.'"

"Right." I kept looking down at my hands, which I was wringing together like a crazy woman. "What I'm trying to say is that...my paper isn't really printed out. It's on my computer, right now."

"I understand the mechanics of a printer, young lady. Your question?"

"Yes, Sir." Per my norm, I couldn't seem to get out of my own head. "I'm working on my thesis for my master's, Master Mister Brogan."

"Really? Your thesis is on this topic and you don't understand the very basic norms." The irritation in his tone made me wince. "Just Master Lex."

"Sorry. Got it." I could've died from the shame I was feeling, but there were no rocks to get under, no trees to hide behind, and no escape route to run to. So, I took a deep breath, hoping to focus my thoughts on something sane and understandable. What to ask that would redeem me in his eyes? "Like I told you, Master Lex, the title of my paper is—"

"I've heard enough about your thesis already." He narrowed his eyelids and tilted his head slightly forward, a clear message that his patience was thinning.

"Okay. I'm thinking."

"And I'm waiting."

I lost my head. He was demanding a question. I blurted the first thing that came to my mind. "How good are you at spanking?"

His eyebrows shot up and then immediately came down. The corners of his sexy mouth turned up ever so slightly. My cheeks burned and my eyes watered. I'd never been so embarrassed in all my life. The students behind me began giggling.

Master Lex's lips thinned, and he glared at the other attendees. Instantly, the room was as still as a morgue.

Dr. Vickers smiled broadly, which stunned me. I didn't know she had any humor in her. I wasn't sure how I would ever face her again after my inappropriate outburst. Of all the things I could've asked the man, I chose to place both my feet directly into my gaping maw.

"Mister Bro...I mean Master Lex, I-I didn't mean—"

"Quiet, Front Row."

I snapped my mouth shut and felt a shiver shoot up and down my spine.

"Your question is valid." He nodded. "Yes. I'm excellent at that activity. It's one of my specialties. It is the reason I chose 'The Spanking Bench' as the name of my podcast."

"T-Thank you," I choked out.

"You're welcome." He chuckled, and then looked past me. "Next question."

The room erupted in a slew of inquiries, but I couldn't follow a single word. All that ran through my head was a little reenactment movie of what had just occurred.

What kind of woman asks this mountain of hotness if he was good at spanking?

Me, the blubbering idiot, of course.

As I relived his answer, over and over, about spanking being one of his specialties, wild sensations sparked hot inside my body, arousing me to an uncomfortable state. Someone asked another question, but I really didn't hear it. I was watching Master Lex's hands. I tried to calm down, realizing that if I didn't, my pussy would be dripping wet right in the middle of the lecture hall with Master Lex less than five feet in front of me.

I don't know how long the session went on. More than an hour, I'm sure. As he continued answering much better phrased questions, I felt a whirlwind of thoughts blow through me. My first idea was to beeline for the exit the second the lecture ended, but then I decided against it. I wasn't about to give Dr. Vickers the satisfaction of seeing me cower. She'd obviously invited me to this lecture expecting me to fail. But though I'd lost the battle at the beginning of Lex's talk, I wasn't about to lose the war. Besides, I needed to interview people who actually practiced BDSM, and Master Lex fit that bill perfectly. And he owned The Cell. If I got access, with Master Lex's blessing, to his BDSM club, the members there might actually be receptive to answering some of my questions. Hell, some might even agree to fill out my survey. So, I stayed put in my chair on the front row after the talk was over, trying to muster the courage to approach him.

Several of the students came up to Master Lex after. When one of the long-legged co-eds touched his forearm, jealousy burst hot inside me, but I kept my reaction hidden by looking back at my hands in my lap.

As the last attendee left the room, I suddenly felt like I'd made a mistake by staying. Dr. Vickers, Master Lex, and I were the only ones left. When he turned his gaze back to me, I immediately knew I should've gone with my first thought of bolting from the room. Too late.

"Do you have another question for me?" He moved around the podium and stood less than a foot in front of me.

I looked over at Dr. Vickers, who seemed to be studying my every move. Then I turned back to him and stood up. "Yes, Sir. I have a question for you."

"Trouble getting to the point, I see. What is your question, little sub?"

"Oh." Him calling me "little sub" thrilled me, but I knew I had to set him straight. "You see, I'm not a practitioner of BDSM. I'm only researching the lifestyle. It's for my thesis."

Lex looked at Dr. Vickers. "Here we go again, Em."

She nodded. "I told you, Lex."

Apparently, Master Lex and Dr. Vickers were friends and had held some kind of discussion about me.

He cupped my chin, and I became dizzy. "Stand up."

Unable to raise any resistance inside me, I obeyed.

His blue eyes seemed fathomless to me. "I've heard enough about your thesis. Ask me?"

I gulped. "Would you consider letting me inside your club?"

He stared at me for the longest time as though considering something. Or perhaps he was just giving me time to get really uncomfortable. It worked. By the time he spoke, my stomach was in knots.

"My club is very selective," Master Lex explained in that deep rumble of his. "You just told me that you're not interested in experiencing its particular fruits. That's a deal breaker."

Heat flashed through me. "That isn't exactly what I said."

"Petulant, isn't she?" Dr. Vickers asked him.

Master Lex ignored that comment, preferring to pin me with his eyes. "It is what you said, little one."

"My name is Mia Weiss."

"Nice." With his hand still on my chin, he turned back to Dr. Vickers. "Could you shut the door, Em?"

I wondered why he wanted the door shut, but didn't dare ask him.

She answered, "Sure thing."

When I heard the door latch, my skin tingled on the back of my neck and my anxiety inflated. I braced for what he had in store for me next.

Dr. Vickers leaned against the door from the inside. No one else would be let in. "All secure."

These two knew each other extremely well, which I found odd. How had they met? Were they friends or just associates? That didn't make sense to me. I'd read Dr. Vickers' bio on the university website to try to get some insight into what it would take from me to get her on my side. There was no mention of anything that would've had them crossing paths.

With his hand still on my chin, Lex took a fistful of my long hair in his other hand. He tugged slightly, pulling me from my thoughts. "You're somewhere else. I want you here. Focused."

"Yes, Sir." My pussy ached and my knees turned wobbly.

His hold on my hair changed from tugging to stroking, and I was getting so very wet. "You want in my club, little sub?"

Unable to find words to answer him, I just nodded.

"I need proof that you really deserve access to The Cell. You want in, then for start, pull your pants down to your ankles, right now."

"What?" I couldn't quite comprehend what he was asking—not asking—*commanding*. Had I misheard him?

"That's the deal." He stopped stroking my hair, and stepped back a bit but still within easy reach of me. Then he shamelessly scanned my body, causing my thoughts to jumble. "In or out? What's it going to be, Mia?"

My jaw dropped, but he pushed it back up with his hand.

"Keep your lips together for me." Master Lex touched my cheek, and I tingled from the inside and out. His nostrils flared as he inhaled deeply. He smiled broadly. "I like your scent."

"I'm not wearing any perfume."

"I know." He frowned. "I'm waiting for your answer, but I won't wait much longer. In or out?"

My palms were clammy and my heart thudded in my chest. "You're kidding?"

"I never kid." His tone told me that his patience had fled.

"Can't we work this out another way...?" I needed some advantage to get my footing again. Hoping to impress him that I was truly serious, I added, "...Sir?"

Another tug by him on my locks made me get even hotter, and my clit tingled in my jeans. Clearly, he was testing me and I wasn't about to blow it like I'd done with my ridiculous question earlier. I unbuttoned the top button of my jeans, but then I remembered that Dr. Vickers was leaning against the door. I froze.

"You're stalling, Mia."

"Please. I need a second." I shifted my eyes from Lex and looked directly at Dr. Vickers.

She stared back at me with her unblinking eyes. I'd never thought of her as someone of the Indigo Girls persuasion, but I must've been wrong.

"Your second is up. Again, you have me waiting. That's not helping your cause to get into my club."

I needed in his club. It was the first opening I'd had since I'd begun my thesis. But it was more than my paper that had me willing to comply with his demand. It was Lex himself. His strength of will, intelligence, and demeanor had all of me, inside and out, intrigued. I wanted to impress him. And if I got in his club, I would get to spend more time with him. There wasn't anything more appealing to me at that moment than that last possibility.

"What the fuck," I said, hoping to sound confident.

His eyes narrowed. "That's not the way a good sub talks, Mia. You take this first step into my world and I will have to punish you for letting those lush lips of yours say such bad words."

Imagining him spanking my ass sent me over the edge. I closed my eyes, bent my knees, and lowered my jeans to my ankles.

His eyes never leaving mine, he ordered, "Now, the panties, Mia."

This whole experience with Master Lex was playing out like a Fellini film. "B-But...you didn't—"

"Panties! Now!"

I obeyed immediately. My clit ached as the air of the room hit it full on. Being so exposed, so vulnerable had tears streaming from my eyes.

When I saw the wet spot on the front of my baby blue panties, I felt the blood rush into my cheeks.

As I'd expected, he looked directly at the center of my underwear around my ankles. He knew how turned on I was. He touched my cheeks with his fingers.

"I'm sorry, Sir."

Lex smiled. "Tears? So sweet and innocent. The Cell might be too much for you, little sub."

The gravity of what he was offering me—a chance to experience what I'd dreamed about for years—flattened me. My thoughts, normally whizzing and scattered, began to focus with a clarity I didn't know possible.

"I'll make you proud, I promise."

His eyes widened, and then he shook his head. "Fuck. You're going to be so much trouble for me, Mia."

"Please. I did what you asked. Can't I come to your club, Sir?"

He covered my mound with his hand, and I moaned. "Pubic hair?" His tone was softer, but still firm and so very sexy.

"Yes, Sir." Though I knew that many sexually active women shaved their pussies for their lovers, I'd never bothered since bedroom games weren't part of my routine. If I'd known how the lecture from Master Lex was going to end up, I would've made sure to be properly groomed for him.

"You're so wet. Nice."

I realized that Dr. Vickers had just been given more ammo against me. Though I couldn't see her, she could definitely see me. How would I ever be able to face her again? My cheeks were hot enough to fry eggs. The only answer was for me to transfer to another university come tomorrow morning.

"Eyes on me, sub." Lex wasn't about to let me forget that he was in charge. "Quiet that mind of yours, understand?"

I nodded and stared straight into his eyes, drowning in his deep blue stare. Dr. Vickers seemed so distant and forgotten. No man had ever overwhelmed me like Lex. Right then, the uncontrollable cravings to be with this man, this Master, this steamroller exploded inside me like wild fire.

Once again, he tugged on my hair. "I'm not sure you have it in you for my ways."

If I didn't act now, the man and his offer would be lost to me. "Please, Sir. Give me a chance."

He released his grip on my locks. "Bend over."

Was he going to spank me? I held my breath, hoping he might.

"When you arrive at my club tomorrow night, sub, have your pussy shaved." Lex slapped my ass with his open hand.

I yelped from the sting in the center of my bottom.

He walked over to Dr. Vickers and turned back. "Pants up, Front Row."

"Yes, Sir." I pulled them up as my entire body vibrated.

"What's your cell number, Mia?"

I rattled it off instantly.

"I'll send you a text with instructions."

"Yes, Sir."

Lex sent me a toothy smile, and I melted into a puddle. He and Dr. Vickers left me alone without another word.

It's 2:35AM and I can't quiet my mind enough to fall asleep, diary.

Tomorrow night I get to walk into The Cell and see Master Lex again.

I'm so excited!

Jan 3rd

❧✿❧

The texts from Lex came early this morning. I won't lie. I sat at my table, cup of coffee in hand, watching the damn cell phone until it buzzed. I read those little fuckers as fast as he could send them. Each text was a set of instructions I was to follow before arriving at the club. I completed every one of them exactly as he'd ordered.

The first thing he wanted me to do was decide on a couple of safe words. I was proud to have already written a bit on the topic in my paper, having read books and videos on the lifestyle. The first word he wanted me to come up with would reduce the level of intensity of the play. The other word would stop it all together. Once I had chosen my two words, I moved onto his next instructions.

His second order was to watch a video on a specific website. It was an instructional demonstration on how to shave your vagina. Though I was tempted to watch the first installment, which was a demonstration of a Dom defuzzing his sub, I didn't.

Lex had been clear that I was to watch the self-shaving segment only.

I began the process of eliminating my pubes on my own. Still, I imagined what it would be like to have Master Lex grooming my pussy.

I trimmed my hair with scissors, following the video's first step.

Next, I took a warm bath, rubbing my pussy with a cloth to soften what was left of my hair. Lifting my right leg up on the edge of the tub, my hands began to shake as desire shot through me.

I had to take several deep breaths to calm myself. When I applied the shaving gel, the memory of Lex covering my mound whirled in my mind. My heartbeat raced, hoping he would touch me again down there tonight and would be satisfied with my work. I put my fingers in my pussy's flesh and held the right side taut, shaving it with the sharp razor. Making sure I went in the same direction as my pubes grew, I took it slow and easy.

I slipped back into the warm water when I was finished removing all my pussy's hair. I wiped the remaining lather with a cloth and shivered as wicked thoughts buzzed in my head. I was so aroused I considered getting out my vibrator, but I didn't. I still had more of Lex's directions to get through.

Next, I went to an address he'd sent me. It was a BDSM shop, and I was to pick up an outfit he'd chosen for me for the evening.

I walked in. It was unlike any boutique I'd ever been in. The walls were black. All the tables were made of chrome. On the tables were a wide variety of paddles, restraints, and other toys I didn't recognize. There were racks of BDSM outfits. Leather and latex hung around the room on long rods. There was also what looked more like costumes to me—military garb, nurses' uniforms, pirate outfits, princess dresses, and more.

"May I help you?" The woman behind the counter had the most beautiful tats on her arms. Her hair was cut chin length like the woman who played the kick-ass vampire in that blockbuster 3-D movie.

"I hope so."

"Newbie?" she asked.

I shrugged. "Lex Brogan sent me."

"Ah. Mia." She grinned and pulled out a large package. It reminded me of something you would get from a fine department store after you'd purchased something quite expensive. "I'm Vivian. Here's the outfit he ordered up for you, doll. You're all set for tonight."

"What do I owe you?"

"You are new." The woman chuckled. "It's on Master Lex's bill. Have fun."

"Thank you, Vivian." I took the box and rushed out the door.

There wasn't a hint of uncertainty in Lex's next instructional text. "Do not open the package until you are home, sub."

By the time I finally walked through my front door, I was trembling with anticipation. Though I was expecting something more provocative, I was thrilled with the outfit he'd chosen for me.

The blue gingham-print dress with its ruffled hemline and lace trim, harkened to an earlier age where innocence was the norm. Two little straps, also of the same print, would leave my shoulders exposed. I found a satin ribbon inside that Lex had instructed me to use to tie my hair up into a ponytail. Also in the box was a pair of white thigh-high stockings with satin bows on the top of each. Finishing out my costume for the evening at The Cell were platform pumps with round closed toes and straps. He'd been very specific that I wasn't to wear any panties.

I dressed, vibrating from head to toe. I applied some blush to my cheeks, the only makeup he would allow. When I looked at my reflection in the mirror, I gasped. I looked like I'd just stepped off the bus from Kansas. I couldn't help but giggle a little at myself. My image screamed farm girl.

I had finished all Lex's orders by the time the limo he'd sent to take me to The Cell showed up.

The driver wore a uniform, including a chauffeur hat. The tag on his jacket lapel let me know his name was Dominick. He didn't say much. With his six-foot-six height and bulging muscles, Dominick looked more like a bodyguard than a chauffer. As he escorted me from my apartment to the car door, I wondered if my neighbors were peering out from their windows. I felt like a princess. The stretch limo was pearl white. The passenger compartment would easily seat ten. Inside I was impressed to find a TV, Blu-ray, neon lights, and a privacy partition. The wet bar had water, sodas, juices, and ice but no booze, which I thought odd.

Dominick drove us to the front of the club. A long line of patrons wrapped around the building. There were two linebacker-sized bouncers manning the way inside. They were letting in only a few people at a time.

The driver didn't stop there, but drove around to the side, which was blocked by a large metal gate. He punched some buttons on the console and the barrier opened. When the limo stopped by a side door, I tried to open the door, but it didn't budge.

"Miss, Master Lex will be escorting you inside. I just sent him a text that we are here."

"Okay. Thank you for driving me here."

"My pleasure."

I waited in the car, fiddling nervously with the lace on my dress. Time seemed to slow to a crawl. Then I saw Lex march out the side door. He was in a dark suit, white shirt, and red tie. Though I'd half expected him to be in something leather like the Dom outfits I'd seen at the boutique earlier, he still looked like sex-on-a-stick to me.

My need to be spanked by him was so intense that butterflies fluttered wildly inside me. I'd been thinking about his hand on my ass ever since I'd obeyed his order and pulled my panties down around my ankles in the lecture hall. I needed his spanking. I wanted his spanking. And tonight, I was going to get his spanking.

Lex went to the front of the limo and spoke to the driver first. Since the privacy partition was up, I couldn't hear what they said to each other. Then he opened my door.

"Welcome, Mia." He extended his hand for me to take.

I stepped out. "Thank you, Sir."

Next to him, I felt so tiny and feminine, especially in the outfit he'd chosen for me. Was I really going through with this? It was hard for me to believe that I was hoping to have my bare bottom spanked by him. But I was—very much so.

"What's your safe word to cool things down?"

"Sugar."

"Got it. And to stop the play?"

"Freeze." Something about having that bit of fail-safe felt good to me, but I would do my best not to utter it to him. Still, I felt a tinge of hesitation spring to life inside me.

"Good choices, sub. When we go inside, you are not to look at anyone in the eyes or acknowledge anyone or respond to anyone until I say so. You are to follow my every command. You are not to question me. Do you understand, Mia?"

"Yes, Sir." Would my fantasy mirror the reality that lay ahead for me? I wasn't sure, but looking into his deep, blue eyes, I knew there was no turning back now.

"Excellent. Time for you to experience my club."

We walked through the door of The Cell and two more muscled bouncers were inside. They were dressed in prison-guard uniforms, enhancing the theme of the club, I guessed. I made sure not to look them directly in the eye, but I could almost feel their lurid stares on my skin.

We walked down one hallway filled with doors spaced twenty feet apart. This place was massive, much larger than it appeared from the outside. On each door was a number. I wondered what was inside, but didn't ask. Then we turned left into another hallway. And another left brought us to a wider space. There were large panes of glass that looked into the rooms that the numbered doors went into. People stood at the windows, gawking at the activity that was going on inside. A man and a woman stared through the window to our left. They were wrapped in each others arms, watching intently.

Lex stopped and gestured to the scenes. "Indulge your curiosity, Mia. Take a look."

"Thank you, Sir." I walked up to the glass nearest us and peered into the room. It looked like a doctor's examination room. Well, the deeply perverted version. A naked woman was stretched out face down on the bed. Two men with stethoscopes around their necks were paddling her ass.

I choked back a squeal. Her ass was bright pink, and she was writhing on the sheets.

"You like, honey?" The man watching asked me, keeping his arms around the woman by him.

I nodded, feeling so charged up and hot.

Lex pulled me with a jerk away from the window, and I realized I'd already disobeyed his order by acknowledging the other man. My cheeks burned with shame.

We continued down the maze of hallways until he came to a door with the number fourteen on it. He opened it and directed me inside.

The room didn't look like a room at all. Instead, I had the odd feeling that I'd just stepped onto a deserted highway. There was pavement under my feet—real pavement. The only light came from what appeared to be a crescent moon above me and the large glass pane opposite where I'd entered. I didn't see anyone standing there, but wondered if that would change once I had my ass in the air. I trembled, scared but unwilling to back out.

"Get on that, sub." Lex pointed to the bicycle on my left. He stayed in the doorway.

The bike had been tricked out so that the rider could pedal and it would remain stationary, but it didn't look a thing like the ones I'd seen at the gym. This bike, with its wicker basket hanging from its handlebars, would've been a girl's dream—*a girl from the fifties, at least.* Though it was quite difficult for me to see, I was able to make out an actual police car beyond the bike. No wonder The Cell, with its rooms that would fit on any movie production company's back lot, was frequented by the rich and famous.

I hopped on the bike and looked back at him. "Now what, Sir?"

"Are you still on board?"

This was uncharted territory for me, but I wanted to really explore my fantasies. Still, a bit of hesitation and anxiety remained in the back of my mind, but that only heightened my excitement. "Yes, Lex."

"You will follow this last command. When a policeman tells you to do something, you do it without question."

Weird, but I was game. "I will, but I don't understand what that has to do with anything, Sir."

"Then wait and see, Mia. Wait and see." He closed the door behind him, a resounding thud echoing through the room.

The room's temperature was quite cool, and I began to shiver. From what must have been hidden speakers, the sounds of a country night filled my ears. I heard crickets chirping at first. Then I heard a wolf howling off in the distance. I kept looking back at the door, but Lex never returned. The imagery was doing its magic quite well. I let go of my logic, which knew this was a room in The Cell in the center of the city, and clung to my imagination, which latched onto the idea that I was actually outdoors, far away from civilization. I felt so alone and the wolf's call seemed to be getting closer.

I began peddling as fast as I could. The wind hit my face. Another special effect? Had to be. But the spell was complete, and my heart thudded in my chest. I was so afraid of being alone on this road. Where was Lex? Why had he brought me here?

I heard footsteps behind me. Lex had left from the door near me, not from behind. A seed of panic began to sprout and grow in me.

Suddenly, the red and blue lights of the police car came on.

Relief filled me. Now that the police were here, I would be safe. I stopped pedaling and looked back at the car. The headlights came on, blinding me. Then I heard the clicks of the officer's boots hitting the pavement.

"Eyes forward, miss." He commanded.

I obeyed, thinking the policeman sounded a bit like Lex. Was he masking his voice to enhance the experience or had he sent another Dom in to teach me a lesson?

"Why are you out on this road alone at this hour, young lady? Shouldn't you be at home?" he asked.

Try as I might, I couldn't be certain that this was Lex. The tone and inflection was the same, but there was a drawl that I hadn't heard from him before. Trepidation inched through me, but beyond the nerves was a need to explore.

"I'm not sure where I am, Officer."

The guy came up next to me, but I only glanced at him from the corner of my eye. His leather boots and wrinkle-free uniform were the blackest black. He wore mirrored Aviator sunglasses, which I thought strange since it was night. The cop was the same height as Lex, but so were the bouncers I'd met when I came into The Cell. This guy could be anyone.

"You know how dangerous it is for someone sweet and innocent like you to be out here?" His hand came down on my shoulder and squeezed.

"Yes, Sir," I choked out. "I won't do it again."

"How can I be sure about that?"

"I promise. I won't go out on this road again unless it's light outside, Officer."

"Not good enough, little sub."

Lex had called me that in the lecture hall. Once I believed it was him, tingles began to dance on my skin.

"Off the bike, miss."

I complied, and then he grabbed me by the arm and led me to the back of his car with its lights still flashing.

"Bend over the trunk, young lady. You have to learn your lesson."

His words went deep into me. My pussy moistened, and my body shook from head to toe. I tried to stretch onto the trunk's lid, but couldn't. I was too short for my middle to reach its bend.

"On your tiptoes, miss."

He took control of the situation, leaving not an inch of wiggle room. He did it so forcibly and with such natural confidence that I felt something deep inside me open. The door to that secret place inside me had cracked open before, but I had the feeling that this man could open it wide. My door might not close again after he was done with me. Something about this moment let me just *be*.

Once I did as he'd instructed, I was able to press my breast and crotch into the cool metal.

He pulled up my dress, and I felt the blood race to my face. "No panties?"

"B-But you told me to not wear them..."

"I told you?"

"Well...a man...Lex..." My mind stirred with doubt. Could I have been mistaken? Could this be another Dom he'd sent to spank me? Of course it could be. I'd been so foolish. I tensed. "Perhaps this is not—"

"Quiet! You deserve this, little sub. You know you do."

The cop had to be Lex, but I wasn't absolutely certain.

Though the tiniest bit of doubt remained, I decided to go through with the bare-bottomed spanking that Lex had set up for me, whether or not this man was him or not. Foolish? Probably. But I didn't want to disappoint Lex.

"Are you ready for your punishment?"

"Yes, Sir." My heartbeat raced in my chest as his hands cupped my ass.

"Don't move." I watched the cop walk to the side door of his car. He opened it and pulled out a pair of handcuffs and what looked to be a nightstick, only lighter and flexible. "Put your hands over your head, miss."

I nodded and obeyed.

He locked the metal cuffs on my wrists, attaching them to a rod that stuck out of the back window of the car. Apparently, the vehicle had been modified to accommodate the kind of activity I was about to experience. I liked the feel of the metal. I tested the cuffs, wiggling my wrists a little. Nothing. I wouldn't be moving anytime soon.

"I'm going to enjoy beating your pretty little ass, miss." He sounded so brutal and dangerous.

I wondered if this would play out the way I'd imagined since leaving the lecture hall or if I would hate every bit of it.

Then I felt the sting of the first whack from the man's stick. It stung, but only a little. Then another whack fell on my ass, followed by another. Whack. Whack. They were firm but not as hard as I knew I could take. Still, the first spanks made my ass burn. I chewed on my lower lip and fought back tears. I writhed against the police car's cool metal.

"So, you can take more." The cop patted my ass gently with his open hand. "Good to know."

Then he rained rapid-fire blows to my bottom. Spank. Spank. Spank. The heat and ache grew, but he seemed to be intentionally smacking my ass in different spots, moving up and down its flesh.

"That's a pretty pink ass, sub. Really gorgeous."

I heard him toss the stick to the ground. Then I felt him slap my ass with his large, open hand.

Whack. Whack. Whack.

My body bucked and gyrated in sync to each whack. The sound of the spanking echoed in my ears, and he increased his speed. It was a strange song, and we were making it together.

Smack. Smack. Smack. Smack. Smack. Smack. Smack. Smack.

My punishment went on and on until the tears flew from my eyes and my pussy juices spilled onto the trunk. My clit throbbed, and I writhed under his assault. Intense desire and wild sensations rolled through me.

My breathing was labored, and every nerve ending in my body sparked alive. I wanted to prove I could do this, take this, and endure his worst.

The cop stroked my ass in a way that clearly let me know that he would handle me however he saw fit. Still, the gentleness in his fingers' touches as he stroked my bottom reassured me that he wouldn't harm me beyond what I needed or could tolerate.

"Almost done, little sub. Ten more. I want you to count them out aloud for me. Understand?"

"Yes, Sir." I was glad it was only going to be ten. Any more would've been overwhelming.

The pain that he'd built up in my ass was reaching the point where I wouldn't be able to bear much more. Ten would be difficult, but I vowed to try, though my safe word vibrated on my lips. I wanted to prove to Lex, whether he was in the role of the cop or looking in from the hallway window, that I had earned my way into his club fair and square. I'd never craved anyone's approval in my whole life more than Lex's.

Smack.

"One, Sir!" I shouted.

Three more came down, each a little harder than the one before.

"Two! Three! Four, Sir!" My mind drifted into a dizzy, warm place. The worries of my thesis, my bills, and my life faded away with each whack of his hand to my ass. All that was left was my body and its responses to the punishment by this policeman.

"Five! Six! Seven!" I couldn't keep still. My ass was on fire. Every inch of my body shook. My climax was so very close.

Smack. Smack.

I counted them as he'd commanded. Then came the final spank from him. It was harder than all that had come before, and the collision of his hand to my ass was explosive, calling forth the most powerful orgasm I've ever had in my life. His hand came between my legs, and pressed on my puffy folds.

When his thumb pressed gently on my clit, I screamed, "Yes! God, yes!"

My body melted into the car as my womb convulsed again and again. Using his hands and his lips alone, the officer kept the intensity of my climax hot and high. The swipes of his tongue on my lower back and the pressure of his fingers on my pussy and clit fanned my flames over and over. Each time I thought the ride was over, another tender touch or intimate kiss sent me flying.

He unlocked the cuffs, removing them from the rod in the back window. I thought he was going to take them completely off me, but instead, he left them dangling on my right wrist.

"Roll over on your back, miss."

Unable to resist, I complied. The helmet was gone but his glasses remained. The illusion swamped my brain into acceptance. I was on a lonely road with a cop who had rescued me from harm or maybe even death. I owed him my very life. I had sunk completely into the fantasy, my own troubles gone.

His mouth covered my mound, sending an electric sensation through every inch of my body. His hands held my thighs wide, and he slurped up my juices, driving me mad with desire. I had to be filled up, possessed, taken.

"Please, officer. I need you." My hands shot to his shoulders, still under the fabric of his uniform. The cuff on my right wrist hung down his back.

"You've taken your punishment very well, sub." His voice thundered from his chest at a deep octave. "I suppose I should reward you for that."

"P-Please."

The cop removed his hands and lips from me, standing tall. He unbuckled his belt, lowering it and the gun it holstered to the ground. Then he pulled his pants down to his boots, revealing white briefs that didn't have any way of hiding his monstrous dick underneath. My jaw dropped as he stripped off his underwear, freeing his thick, nine-inch beast.

He leaned forward and hoisted me off the car and into his arms as if I weighed nothing at all. The officer's brute strength amazed me. I wrapped my legs around his waist and my arms around his neck. The man was built like a fortress of muscles. Any woman would feel completely safe walking beside him.

I stared at my own reflection in his mirrored sunglasses. My hair was in a ponytail, and my face was flush. Before now, I'd never felt more feminine or wanton.

"Time to fill up your pretty cunt with my dick, miss." He lowered me back on the car.

As I watched him don a condom over his massive shaft, a bit of relief rushed through me. I shouldn't have been anxious, though, since I knew from what I'd read about the club earlier that condoms were required. Then he lifted me back into his arms and I wrapped my arms and legs around him again. I felt the head of his cock touch my pussy, and I got even wetter.

Urges ignited inside me, and I shifted my hips, trying to coax him in. The cop jerked me up several inches.

"You've got so much to learn, little sub." His voice had an edge of threat in it. "Stop trying to take charge or else. Understand?"

I couldn't help but grin a bit, longing for more of the "else" from his hand to my bottom. "Yes, Sir."

He kissed my forehead, and I moaned into his throat. A shiver ran up and down my spine as he lowered me down again. This time, his cock split my folds. I obeyed him, trying to remain still though my body was racked with a million vibrations.

My lips trembled as he slowly lowered my weeping sex onto his erect dick, igniting more desire with every stroke forward. His cock was so long and so hard and so wide. I'd never had anything that big inside me. I felt stretched to the very limit, and trying to hold on, I scrapped the back of his neck with my fingernails.

"Squeeze my dick with your pussy, Mia."

I obeyed and tightened my channel around his thickness as he continued thrusting deep into my pussy. With each stroke, his weight pressed on my clit, enhancing my crazed suffering.

"Feels so good," I panted, unable to stay quiet.

"You like me fucking you, sub?"

"Oh, yes!"

"You want me to keep fucking you?"

"Please. Fuck me. Don't stop." Involuntarily, my pussy convulsed on his cock, harder than before.

Like the spanking he'd given me on the back of his cop car, the thrusts of his cock deep into my pussy had me teetering on the edge of pain and pleasure. My moans soon became screams. I couldn't keep still. It was as if my body had a mind of its own, thrashing against him as he held me off the ground and on his dick.

"Oh, God!" The only thing I could focus on was the wild sensations inside my flesh. With each powerful stroke he sent into me, my womb tightened, relaxed, and tightened again, over and over.

"Come for me, little sub." His tone was lower, guttural. "Come now!"

If my mind didn't know he was in charge, my body sure did. Like a glass shattering into a million pieces, I climaxed that instant and everything went kablooey inside me.

"Y-Yesss!" I screamed and hissed. My womb convulsed and my tears burned.

"Fuck! I'm fucking you, sub!" he growled.

He pounded his cock into me, grunting and cursing with each thrust. Then I felt him stiffen with one final plunge into my wet pussy.

"Ahhh!" he yelled, as he came inside me.

Completely spent, I could barely hold onto consciousness as the cop hoisted me up off his cock. I leaned into his chest as he pulled me up in his arms, my legs dangling. Since the cop car's door was still open, he placed me inside in the back.

He took the handcuffs off me. "Stretch out, miss."

Keeping my eyes open, which I found difficult as weariness set in, I did as he'd instructed. He pulled up his uniform pants and put his gun belt back on.

"Did you learn your lesson, miss?"

I smiled and nodded back at the cop. He was still wearing the sunglasses that hid his eyes from me.

"Roll over on your stomach for me."

I obeyed, and was rewarded with a cool ointment to my aching ass. It felt wonderful.

"All done. Flip around, miss."

He tugged on my dress so that it once again covered my pussy. Then he placed a warm blanket that he'd gotten from the front seat on top of me.

"Lex?"

"Shh. Goodbye, Mia." He closed the door, leaving me alone.

I'd convinced myself that the policeman was actually Lex, but now I wondered. Could I have made a mistake? But was it really a mistake? Maybe he was testing me? There was so much I needed to learn about BDSM. As the throbbing of my ass continued, I knew that my first night at The Cell had changed me forever. Deep inside me was something that responded to being spanked. It took me to a place of frenzy and dizziness, a place of craze and deliciousness, a place of bliss and rest. I'd only scratched the surface for my thesis, and I needed more. Would Lex let me come again? Would he let me interview him? There was so much to work out, but the fading vibrations in my body from my climax gently rocked me, dulling my thoughts. Though I tried to remain awake, I did finally drift off to sleep.

"TIME TO GO HOME, MIA." Lex's command woke me.

I opened my eyes, and saw he was wearing the suit I'd seen him in earlier. His steely blue eyes were unblinking and made me shiver.

How long had I slept in the back of the cop car? I had no idea, but my sleep was at the deepest level, the place where the concept of time has no hold. I might've been out for only a minute, but it could've been hours, too.

"Did you change?" I asked, hoping he had. If not, then the cop had been some other guy.

"Did I not make myself clear, sub?" The edge in his tone worried me. I had felt so close to the cop. I didn't feel close to this man. Could he have changed so much?

"What?"

"Time. To. Go. Home."

Though I wanted to mentally compare the phrasing and tone that the cop had used to Lex's, I found myself leaping from the car like a little soldier following the orders of his commander. I stood beside him and gazed into his gorgeous eyes.

"Better, little one."

"May I come back to your club, Lex? I did what you asked."

"Yes, you did."

"Ask the officer," I said, hoping to spot a clue from his reaction. But none came. I found no change in him. Not one. His eyes never blinked, and he stood as still as a statue. "I deserve to come back, Lex."

"You think so?" His lips curled up, making me weak in the knees. "Well, I'll think about it."

"Please?"

"I like that you know how to beg, but you need to learn when it works and when it doesn't, sub."

I felt like I was blowing my chance for a repeat visit to The Cell. I needed to switch tactics with Lex, but wasn't sure how.

He reached into the backseat of the vehicle and pulled out the blanket. Wrapping it around me, he led me out the door. I turned and took a long look back at the scene.

"You've got quite the setup here at your club." I sighed, recalling the spanking the officer had given me. "You should be very proud of what you've created here."

His eyes widened as if I'd hit some kind of nerve in him. He stared at me for the longest time. He finally shook his head. "You're such a sweet treasure, pet. I didn't know a woman like you even existed in the world."

I wasn't entirely sure that was a good thing. "What do you mean by that?"

"Enough talk. You're exhausted. You need rest since you're coming back tomorrow."

Totally thrilled that he was going to allow me back in the club, I nodded. With my hand in his, Lex led me out of the club the same way we'd come in.

The limo was idling by the side door with the driver standing by.

Lex opened the door for me. "I'll text you with instructions for tomorrow night, Mia, just like I did today."

"Thank you."

Suddenly, he grabbed me by the back of the neck and pulled me in for a kiss. His mouth crashed against mine, and I melted into him. As his tongue swept past my lips, I became wonderfully woozy.

And just as fast as the kiss had come, it ended, leaving me wanting more.

"Goodnight, little sub."

Jan 4th

L ike yesterday, I sat and waited, the day not quite beginning until
my phone chimed. Lex's first text came early and with his very
specific instructions.

*Breakfast will arrive shortly. Don't pick at it. Eat until you are full. You'll
need you're strength tonight.*

It felt amazing to have someone take care of every detail of my day.

Fifteen minutes after I'd first read the text, there was a knock on
the door. Right on time.

The delivery girl handed me the packages with the delicious breakfast inside. I could smell a dozen culinary aromas like bacon, eggs,
honey, bananas, strawberries, and so much more, causing my stomach
to growl.

"Let me get you a tip after I put these on the table."

She shook her head. "No tip. Strict instructions from your
husband."

I thought about correcting her, but didn't. She wouldn't care one
way or the other. But her calling him my *husband* got my mind
buzzing. What was he to me? I'd only met him recently, but now I was
following his every direction. I still thought that the cop and Lex
were the same, but I wasn't totally sure. If not, I hadn't even had sex

with Lex. I couldn't call him *my* Master. I knew that to be more of a formal act in the BDSM community. And yet, I couldn't refuse him anything. I'd known it that first meeting when I'd pulled my panties down to my ankles in the lecture hall. And it wasn't just being in the same room that turned me into soft clay in his hands. Even his texts unhinged me so much that I could not resist his words on my cell's screen.

"Do you need anything else?" she asked, smiling broadly.

"No. This is fine. Thank you for bringing this to me."

"My pleasure."

I closed the door, and per Lex's instructions, I ate the meal he'd sent. Try as I might, I couldn't finish it. I doubted that a family of ten would've been able to. Every bite had been delicious and satisfying.

The next text came, and the next.

Each and every one, I followed to the letter. And every time I completed one of his tasks, I grew prouder of myself and more excited about the evening he had in store for me.

There was another knock on my door.

Thanks to the most recent of Lex's texts, I knew the person knocking was Vivian, the woman I'd met at the BDSM boutique yesterday.

I opened the door. "Come on in."

"Hi, Mia." She grinned and handed me the box in her hands. "Did you have fun last night?"

Fun didn't begin to cover it. I'd discovered something about myself. I was still discovering with every small task. "I did. What kind of outfit does Lex have me in tonight?"

Vivian's lips curved up in a smile. "One of my personal faves, kiddo. A slutty maiden dress that will knock his socks off."

I was glad to hear that. "Do you have time to come in for a cup of coffee, Vivian? I have some questions I'd like to ask you, if you don't mind."

"I heard you are working on a thesis. Until Lex gives the green light, no one is going to talk to you about the life. That includes me. I'm sorry." She gave me a sympathetic look.

I sighed. "No worries."

"That's not to say I won't be talking with you soon. I think you're about the only woman who has ever been able to get under Lex's skin."

The only woman to get under his skin? How could that be possible? I was confused but also foolishly hoping it was true. "You can't tell me that he hasn't been with a lot of women. Maybe even you?" That thought sent a bolt of worry and jealousy through me.

Vivian shrugged. "Not me. Boy, don't think I wouldn't have loved to drink from that fountain if I'd gotten the chance. I'm a bit of a switch, and Lex only goes for pure subs."

Knowing that she'd not been with him filled me with relief. "What do you mean I've gotten under his skin?"

She held up her hands. "I've already said too much. Just whatever you're doing, keep it up. You'll get his green light and get your interviews, I'm sure of it."

"Thanks, Vivian."

"My friends call me, Viv." She winked.

"Viv. Thanks."

"Bye, kiddo. Have fun tonight."

I shut the door and put the box on my sofa. I ripped off the top, revealing the outfit Lex had chosen for me for my second visit to his club. I slipped on the maiden outfit and became both excited and nervous. Was I actually brave enough to show up at The Cell dressed like a...how had Viv described it...slutty maiden?

The dress reminded me of the costumes my sister wore to the Renaissance festivals she'd forced me to go to with her. She was—still is—a huge fan of anything medieval. Actually, my dress resembled her costumes in theme, but not in any other way. Sure, the bodice laced in the front. The lacing was gold and the top was layered with green and brown fabric. A ruffled skirt completed the dress. It harkened to the days of maidens and knights, but its length hit the very top of my thighs, not my knees. The top gaped wide, exposing the cleavage of my over-sized chest. Since, once again, he'd ordered me to go pantyless, my outfit would likely garner me an indecent exposure charge in most states.

I wondered what kind of scene Lex would send me to tonight. I might be a wench in a tavern delivering drinks to one of the king's knights or a gypsy girl telling the fortune of a lost journeyman. What-ever he'd set up, I knew I would have one of the best experiences in my life.

It was hours before the limo was to arrive, so I took the outfit off and placed it on my bed. I wasn't sure how I would pass the time when another of Lex's texts came in.

Another website I was to go to. I got my laptop out and entered in the address. I'd gone to every place on the Internet about BDSM in the past several months—or so I thought. When the page opened, it asked for a username and password. As if Lex had hidden cameras in my apartment and knew what I needed the instant I needed it, his next text came. He'd set up a temporary username and password for me. I entered them, and the page opened.

My jaw dropped. This was a site with more information on BDSM than I knew existed. A directory listed every club in the world, with ratings from users about each. The Cell was rated in the top ten in the world for every category, and was actually number one in several.

Per Lex's text command, I went directly to the link that took me to a specific section on the site that focused only on protocols. The wealth of information was staggering. There were articles, discussion groups, videos, and more. I devoured several. I opened up a notepad on my laptop and entered several quotes I'd found.

The more I read, the more I began to look at BDSM in a new and different way. There was more to the lifestyle than just kink. There was more to it than just sex, too. It had a symmetry and grace that was too easy for an outsider to miss.

I'd learned under Lex's tutoring that my most basic nature was to please, yet being completely open and real didn't come easy. But my tutor knew how to get past my internal barricades. The combination of his demands and punishments cracked my shell, reaching my deepest hidden pleasure spots.

I knew that I would have to change much of what I'd done on my thesis, but I didn't mind. For the first time, I even envisioned finishing it.

Another text came in from Lex.

"Get dressed and be ready to leave in thirty minutes. The driver will be knocking on your door then."

I looked at the clock on my microwave and couldn't believe that hours had past since I'd first received Lex's text about the website. The day had passed quickly, my mind focused on work. I'd gotten everything done I'd needed to do, and without my normal frustrating starts and stops. I closed my laptop, stood up, stretched, and headed to my room.

By the time I heard the knock on the door, I was vibrating from head to toe, anxious to see Lex again.

I opened my door and saw a different driver this time. A woman.

"Hello, Ms. Weiss."

"Hi. Call me, Mia."

The woman nodded and pointed to the limo. It was nearly identical to the one that had come last night, except it was black and not white. I climbed aboard, imagining it was a carriage taking me to the castle of the king. I looked down at my outfit and giggled. Would I be the unknown princess dressed as a lowly maid tonight? Maybe. But whatever Lex had planned for me, I prayed it included his hand, and not another's, on my ass.

We went through the gates at the side of the club, and again, Lex came out to meet me. Tonight, he wore jeans, boots, a T-shirt, and a sport coat. My mouth watered as I watched him walk to the car from the side entrance of The Cell.

He opened the door, looking me up and down like a CT scan. "Excellent."

"I'm glad you like it, Sir." I lowered my eyes in deference to him.

There were nuances I'd learned today on the website about some of the protocols that a casual observer would likely miss, but I wanted to impress him tonight.

He cupped my chin. "Look at me, sub."

I gazed at him and saw him smile. It was enough to send a tingle through my body.

"Same rules as last night, Mia. No talking, looking, or responding to anyone until I say so. Understand?"

It was so much easier now that I really grasped the rules. "Yes, Sir."

"Okay then. Let's go inside for round two." He put his arm around my shoulders and guided me to the side door.

With each step, my temperature rose as I recalled the lecture hall with him and the deserted road with the police officer. I thought about rubbing my ass but didn't. I wasn't sure Lex would want me to touch myself without his permission.

As we walked through the door, I made sure to keep my eyes down or on Lex. We made several turns, going down one hallway after another. There seemed to be more people in the club tonight, but I continued following the protocols I'd read about earlier, looking into no one's eyes save my blue-eyed teacher.

The last hallway was empty, which I found strange at first, until I spotted a sign hanging above: "This section is closed for repairs."

Anxiety and desire swung blows at each other inside my thoughts. My heart pounded the inside of my chest. "Are we alone, Sir?"

He didn't answer but continued leading me down the hall.

At the end of the passage, we came to the last door. It looked ancient and foreboding. I wondered what scene was behind it. I imagined an English manor beyond the dark wood door that was held in place by black metal hinges.

"We're here."

"Where?" Would I play the maid of the estate where Lex was lord? I sure hoped so.

Once again, he didn't answer. He took out a key and unlocked the door. I recalled that the room he'd taken me to last night hadn't been locked. Why was this one? The claws of fear dug into my mind.

As Lex swung the door open, it creaked like the ones in scary movies always did. "Go down the stairs, little sub."

I didn't move, couldn't. I looked beyond the door and could only make out the faintest of lights reflected on the walls. The glow came from below from some source I couldn't see.

As he'd done in the lecture hall, he asked me, "In or out, Mia?"

His blue eyes were somehow brighter tonight. Clearly, he wanted me to go down those stairs to what he'd prepared for me this evening.

Looking at him, I found just enough courage to push my fears aside, though they were still present and clawing at the back of my mind. "Definitely in, Sir. I want in."

He smiled, and then it faded into a scowl. Were his actions all part of enhancing the experience for me? I wondered.

He pointed to the door. "Now."

"Yes, Sir."

I stepped through the door to the landing that led to the stairs below. It curved, hiding whatever the stairs led to.

"I'm impressed, sub. Now, go down the stairs and see what I've set up for you."

I turned back, only to see him shut the door on me. Then I heard the lock engage.

"Sir!"

I pounded on the door, but it remained closed and locked. My misgivings were howling in my ears, bringing up a million possibilities at what was at the bottom of those stairs. Even though my nerves were on high alert, I reminded myself that last night had been an incredible experience—and very safe. Clearly, The Cell was a place of fantasy and sexual exploration with Lex as its proprietor, wicked wizard, and ultimate Master. Besides, I had my safe word that could halt everything once uttered from my lips.

Cautiously, I descended the steps.

Halfway down, I saw the torch—yes, an actual torch. It was the only light in the stairwell. Then I noticed that the walls were not plaster or drywall but were stone. I wondered if the walls were faux, another illusion of The Cell. I reached out and touched them. The cold hit my fingertips, and I shivered. The walls were actual masonry. I looked down at the steps. They were made of stone, too. This was quite an expense to create a fantasy for the club's patrons, but from what I'd already seen, expense was not a problem for its owner.

I took the final steps and came to a large oak door. Not sure if I was to walk in or knock, I chose to take my chances and turned the knob slowly, hoping it wouldn't inform anyone within of my arrival. Luckily, it didn't make a sound. When I opened the door, I scanned the room. Like the stairwell, burning torches in iron sconces on the walls cast a dim light. Still, it was enough for me to get a sense of the room. It screamed of medieval torture. Well, at least I was dressed for the part.

Chains hung from every wall, and on the five wooden tables around the room were what looked to be a wide assortment of paddles, whips, and other implements of punishment. One word came to mind for this room—*dungeon*.

At the center was a wooden set of stocks built in a way that was obviously used to restrain a person in a bent-over position. Clearly, it was for delivering spankings. Though I was trembling with anxiety, I found the thing strangely compelling. I wondered what it would feel like to be locked into the stocks with my ass jutted out for Lex to spank.

I jumped back as two muscular men wearing black leather aprons suddenly appeared in front of me.

"Look, brother. A visitor." The bald man to my right smiled. "How nice for us."

I'd been so mesmerized by the implements of the dungeon, I'd not noticed them standing in the corners. They looked like twins, except that one had long, black hair down to his shoulders and the other one was completely bald. They both sported several tats on their arms. Their eyes looked like caramels.

My jaw dropped. Was I supposed to get spanked by them?

The one with the long hair turned to the other. "Behave, Kane. Hello, Mia."

They'd been expecting me.

"Hello," I squeaked out as uneasiness swelled inside me.

"My name is Reed. We've got the place all ready for you, just as Master Lex requested."

The mention of the club owner's name calmed my nerves, if only a bit. "You're following, Lex's instructions?"

"Of course." The bald guy pointed to the stocks I'd just seen. "That's for you. You're five foot three, yes?"

I nodded, staring at the contraption and feeling my palms get moist.

"That's terrific. I won't need to adjust the pillory to fit you since it's already set to your height."

"Shall we get you set up for the dungeon master, Mia?"

"O-Okay."

Reed asked me what my safe words were, and I told him. Then he sent me a knowing wink. He cleared his throat and then changed his accent. "Dost thou knowest the time, Master Kane?"

"Aye, Master Reed. 'Tis time to chain this comely maiden to the pillory for the Master."

Reed cupped my chin. "Thou are very pretty, dear lady. How fare thee?"

I remembered the way my sister addressed the people at the festivals I'd attended with her. "Good Sir, my state is of little consequence. My Lord has commanded me here. By his permission, I am trusted into your care. Such, indeed, by his order, will we both bend to his will."

I was proud at my attempt to sound authentic in the dungeon. When I looked at the two men smiling broadly, I knew I had more than succeeded.

"Come hither, my lady." Reed held out his hand, and I took it.

He guided me to the pillory.

Kane lifted the top piece of the stocks.

Reed nodded.

I bent over and placed my head and hands in the correct places. Since my dress was so short and I wasn't wearing panties, I instantly realized that at least part of my ass was exposed to the brothers. Though being in such a position unhinged me, I also felt inflamed and more than a little excited.

Reed attached some leather cuffs that were chained to the floor to my ankles. "Hark now, the dungeon master approaches."

Normally, such a masquerade would've seemed comical to me, but not now, not tonight. As the clang of footsteps echoed off the walls behind me, I lost myself to the illusion. No longer was I a modern woman working on her thesis. Instead, the magic of Lex's club had changed me into a maiden in a dungeon about to pay for some infraction or crime of mine.

"Good eve, my Lord," the brothers said in unison.

"Good eve, gentlemen." The voice sounded different yet familiar.

I knew it had to be Lex. That knowledge got me vibrating like a live wire.

Reed continued with, "The maiden awaits thee yonder, Sir."

"Thy work is done here, gentlemen."

Reed answered, "By your leave, My Lord."

I heard him and Kane exit, leaving me alone with Lex.

He grabbed my chin, causing me to gasp.

"Look at me, Mia."

"Yes, Sir." I stared up at my punisher. A leather mask hid most of his face, save his eyes and mouth. Thankfully, the blue eyes gazing back at me were the giveaway. This was the man I'd hoped to see.

He was shirtless, exposing his eight-pack abs. His leather pants were tight, giving me a clear view of the outline of his cock. Even his boots, also black leather, complimented his sheer masculine air.

"Sub, are you ready to receive punishment?"

My eyes felt as big as saucers. "Yes, Master. I'm ready."

"No, you are not. This dress impedes me." His tone was low and threatening.

He walked behind me. In a split second, he ripped the dress off of me, shredding it into a worthless heap of fabric. "Better," he growled.

The air hit my naked skin, and I felt gooseflesh pop up everywhere.

"Now, to your punishment, little sub." I heard him walk over to one of the tables. "This paddle will work just fine on your pretty ass. Tonight, I want you to hold back your cries and your tears for as long as you can, understand?"

"Yes, Sir." I wondered why he would have me do that, but of course, I didn't ask.

As if he had read my mind, Lex added, "By holding back, I'll be able to reach those last bastions of resistance inside you. With my help, they will crumble to dust. I want your full surrender, and tonight, you will give it to me."

He rubbed the paddled against my ass.

"Get intimate with it, sub. Tell me how it feels."

"Cold. Hard." I felt my senses opening.

"And?"

"Dangerous." A thrill went through me.

"Excellent." His first swing came and landed in the middle of my bottom.

Since my ass still ached from the previous night's punishments, I chewed on my lip, wanting to obey his command to not cry out from this added sting. It worked, though some tears did well up in my eyes.

"Very good, sub. Very good."

"Thank you, Sir." Having my ass tortured by Lex might've been considered kinky to most, but for me, being with him this way worked to quiet my mind. There had been no painful past event that had kept my walls up. Instead, my hesitations had always been about my distrust of my own instincts. But Lex knew just what to do to get me out of my head and into a place where I could relax and open up to pleasure.

"We're not done. You understand that?"

"Yes, Sir."

Whack. Whack. Whack. Whack.

The stinging pain to my ass had me fighting back my tears. Still the burn sent sensations to my nipples and my clit until the ache had me thrashing in the stocks.

Whack. Whack. Whack.

"M-Master," I whispered. "Thank you."

My toes curled and my hands became fists. Heat flashed through my body. If I hadn't been held in place by the pillory, I would've fallen from the weakness in my legs.

Lex's lips feathered across my ear, sending a shiver down my back. "You're doing great, Mia."

I felt him rub my ass with his open hand, and my pussy got so very wet.

"Thank you, Sir."

"Can you take more, little sub?"

Could I take more? I wanted so much more. "Yes, Master. More."

"With my hand now, sweetheart. Count them for me."

Spank.

"One." I was trembling from head to toe.

Spank. This one crashed into a different spot on my ass.

"Two." Dizziness overwhelmed me.

Spank. Spank. Spank.

"Three. Four. F-Five." My ass was on fire. Lex's strikes never landed on the same spot twice. Wild sensations grew inside me, and my whirling mind quieted and focused, zeroing in on the orgasm he was building up within me. My pussy clenched and my heart fluttered.

Spank. Spank. Spank.

"S-Six. S-Seven." I took a deep breath, resisting the urge to cry out. "Eight."

I was on autopilot, heading into a dreamy subspace. But something kept holding me back.

Spank. Spank.

Though I'd been hesitant to pull my panties down for him at the lecture hall, I knew that from now on, whatever he asked of me, I would do it without holding back.

"Nine...and...."

"Breathe, Mia."

I obeyed him instantly, sucking in a lungful of air. My shaking didn't subside, but I was able to say, "Ten."

"Your ass is a nice, lovely red, sub. Only a few more and we're done. No more counting. Understand?"

I sighed, having found the last bit of counting next to impossible. "Thank you, Sir."

"The next round is going to come from a crop with a pinch that is sharp and severe. I know you've been fantasizing about tonight all day. Right?"

"Yes, I have." It was as if he knew me inside and out. Even my most inner thoughts, which were difficult for me to articulate, he knew.

He chuckled, the sound rolling over my skin. "While it's happening, part of you is going to hate this crop chomping on your flesh. But I know that another part of you will come alive at the same time, something wild and pleasurable. When we're done, you'll be dreaming about the next time."

Though the crop frightened me some, his reassuring words were lulling me more.

In my preparations for my thesis, I'd garnered quite a bit of technical information, including some on subspace. Once he hit my ass with the crop, I'd be taking the steps on the ever-rising hormone ladder of adrenaline and endorphins. It all made sense to me in a clinical, scientific way. But I soon learned that reading about something and really feeling it were two different things entirely.

"Do you trust me, Mia?" he asked.

Did I trust Lex? I shouldn't. My brain knew it should take longer than a day or two, but my heart and soul had opened up the moment I'd laid eyes on him.

"Yes. I totally trust you."

"Then get ready for a rush like you've never experienced." Once again, he stroked my ass with his open hand.

"Yes, Sir." Eagerness and jitters mixed together as I braced for his promised spanking.

Then the first bites of the crop came crashing on my ass.

Smack. Smack. Smack. Smack. Smack.

Like tiny flaming tongues, the pinches came from the crop one after another. The sweltering in my body grew and grew until I couldn't hold back any longer. Heavy drops fell from my eyes, and I wailed aloud. I'd failed his one request to not cry. Shame burned inside me and held me back from letting go completely.

Smack. Smack. Smack. Smack. Smack.

Then I felt my invisible walls crumble as Lex's torture slipped me into a delicious trance. My total focus was on pleasing him, surrendering to him, and the most prominent of all was on trusting him. All the worries of my daily life faded into nothingness, and what remained were the sensations whizzing through my body.

Lex stroked my ass, applying cream that took away some of the sting. "Poor baby. You did so good."

He removed the restraints on my ankles and lifted the top of the stocks. He took me up in his arms, and I melted into him, resting my head against his chest. I could still feel the earlier bites of the paddle and his hand on my ass. My backside throbbed more than it had ever done before.

"I-I'm sorry I-I cried out, Sir."

"Shh. You did as you were told."

"But, Sir, you told me not to cry out and I did."

"I told you to withhold for as long as you could. You did that. I'm proud of you, little sub."

I could hear his satisfaction. He was pleased with me. It was a balm to my soul. My flesh could throb and ache, but there was a piece of me that simply sighed with pleasure at his tone. "Thank you."

"Now, time for your massage." Lex carried me up the stairs and back to the deserted hallway and then to the doorway opposite the one for the stairs. "I'm going to have to lower you, sweetheart. This is one of my private rooms, and I have to unlock the door. You think you can stand for a second while I do that?"

I nodded.

After he placed me on the ground, keeping one arm around me, he put a key in the doorknob and opened the door. Then he whipped me back up into his arms and carried me into the room.

A professional massage table sat in the center of the space. Along one wall were shelves loaded with towels, oils, and more.

Lex placed me on the cushioned table. "Stretch out and put your face in the cradle, sub."

Though not from a man, I'd had a couple of massages and was familiar with the process. I got into position and waited for his manly hands to rub my tension away.

"I'm going to light some candles, turn on some music, and get the oil warmed up, Mia."

He started on my feet, which were normally ticklish. Not with him. With his fingers, he worked on every part, including each toe.

"You carry a lot of your tension here, baby."

As he hit every tiny ball of pressure in my feet, I knew he was right. "I wear high heels sometimes. I bet that has something to do with it, Sir."

He moved his hands up to my calves. "You've sure got the legs for high heels." His touch made me sigh, and I felt my body relax. "I'm going to finish on your thighs and then I'm going to work on your neck and shoulders. Drift off, sweetheart."

"Yes, Sir." I was glad to doze off.

I'm not sure how long he worked on me, but I awoke several times, feeling him kneading out different areas, applying the warm oils. Then I would drift off again.

"God, you've got the perfect ass, sub." He massaged my bottom until my pussy wept.

The more he touched me, the more aroused I became. My whole body began to warm from the oils and his touch.

"I'm going to fuck your gorgeous ass. Have you tried anal before?"

I tensed. "No, Sir."

"You're going to tomorrow night. You've got to trust me. Understand?"

"Yes, Sir." I felt him apply some lubricant to my backside entrance, and I yelped.

"Breathe, Mia. You've done great."

I exhaled and felt him fingering my hole and kissing my lower back. "Y-You said tomorrow, right?"

"Lots to teach you, little sub. Yes. I'm going to get you to come with my fingers in your ass. Once you graduate from that, I'll let you ride my dick. You're in for one awesome trip, Mia. I promise."

"Yes, Sir." I relaxed, and felt his finger pierce me in my virgin bottom. The sting was hot but not unbearable, though I wondered what his massive dick would feel like in my ass.

He plunged his fingers into my ass until I was thrashing on the massage table. My pussy juices dampened the sheet, and I ground my clit into the cushion.

His hand came down on my ass, grabbing my attention immediately. "Did I give you permission to pleasure yourself, subbie?"

I felt the heat fill my cheeks with shame. "No, Sir."

"That's my girl. I'm so impressed." He said with a hint of awe. That he saw me as such thrilled me.

Continuing his in and out finger barrage on my ass, Lex stroked my pussy with his other hand. I pressed my mound into his calluses. He pressed on my clit with his thumb, sending a sea of shivers through me. He parted my wet folds and sent a finger into my channel.

I groaned as his fingers double penetrated me. I fisted the sheet as his torture went on and on, in and out, painfully slow. The friction of his thumb against my tiny bundle of nerves drove me mad with desire.

"Now you can come. Come for me, Mia."

"Oh God!" I screamed, rocking my hips back and forth into his magical fingers as the sensations built.

"Tomorrow I'm going to be fucking this sweet, tight ass."

Imagining him plowing me with his thick dick sent me over the edge. Sensations zoomed through me as the orgasm thundered and pulsed inside me until my whole body shook. I couldn't have remained still even if I'd tried. I yelled his name again and again. Lex had unhinged me and given me another immense climax. I didn't know if I could ever stand to be without his touch again.

Jan 5th

❦

Diary, I'm afraid that I'm falling fast for Lex. And though I'd like to think he's falling for me as well, I have to face some hard facts.

Sure, he's the most awesome lover I've ever had, but I question whether a man like him is even capable of truly loving someone. And I certainly have to wonder why he would choose me. If I'm not very careful, my heart is going to rip in two when he moves from me on to his next student of BDSM.

I'm staring at his text right now, trembling. Another set of instructions. I wish I could refuse him, but I just can't.

I'm to shave my legs and pussy again. Vivian is to drop off another outfit for me later. He's going to fuck my ass tonight, and that scares me some. His finger stretching me there was one thing, but his dick...? I doubt I'd be able to wrap my fingers around its thickness.

Am I being foolish continuing down this path when I know it's going to end badly? Of course I am, but I can't help myself. Lex has made me feel beautiful and sexy. He provides me with something I've been unconsciously yearning for. I didn't really know what I wanted before I heard his low rumble barking orders to me. When I'm with him, everything makes sense. It's like he's able to take me to a place with no worry, and he does it by pushing me and pushing me until my fears melt away. This clearly is akin to the trust bond that I've read so much about. I do trust Lex. I guess it has something to do with him taking the weight off my shoulders and seeing to my needs in a way no one has ever done before.

Damn it, I should text him back that I'm done and end it with my safe word. That's the sensible thing to do.

But the truth is, I'm scared. I'm scared to go forward. And I'm even more terrified to take a step back.

THE WORRY I wrote about earlier is still inside me, but muted. Though my time with him might only last a little bit longer, I plan on taking whatever he offers. Right or wrong, I want to be with him, really with him, any chance I get. At least he's agreed to let me interview him. That's my only chance to really talk to him about how I'm feeling. But I'm jumping ahead, diary. Back to what happened tonight. It was incredible.

I started out the day scared, but something about his texts calmed and relaxed me. Plus, I loved the outfit he chose for me. It was a naughty-schoolgirl outfit with a plaid scarf, plaid skirt, and even a plaid bra. The white oxford shirt gaped a bit due to my large breasts, but I think he knew it would, which thrilled me.

At least, that was what I told myself as I sat in the backseat of the limo fidgeting. Once again, the chauffeur drove through the gates and parked by the side of the club. We waited for at least thirty minutes, but Lex hadn't arrived. I wondered if he had changed his mind about me. What if the dream of the past few nights had come to an abrupt end? Had he moved on to another? Looking down at my cell and his last instruction, I choked back a tear.

A knock on the glass startled me, and I looked up. The knocker wasn't Lex. Standing on the other side of the window stood Dr. Vickers. My jaw dropped when I noticed what she was wearing—a latex, lace-up teddy that left little to the imagination. She also had on thigh-high boots, a military style hat, and was carrying a whip. Behind her was a man wearing only white briefs and a leather collar with a chain that hooked to Dr. Vickers' belt. I'd never seen a Dominatrix in person before now.

I will admit that seeing Dr. Vickers like that was a revelation. A whole lot of things about the woman suddenly made sense. It was something akin to seeing a wild animal finally in its natural habitat.

She opened the door. "Hello, Mia."

"Umm...hello, Dr. Vickers."

"Here, call me Mistress Em."

I smiled. The title fit. Dr. Vickers did seem right for this life. No wonder she'd approved my topic for my thesis.

"There was some electrical issue in one of the rooms that Lex had to check out. He sent me to fetch you. Come with me."

Relieved that he still wanted to see me, I nodded and stepped out of the car.

With her man in tow, she led me into the club and to the room Lex had chosen for me tonight. The place looked like a college classroom and reminded me a little of the lecture hall I'd met him in.

They guy trailing Dr. Vickers asked, "Mistress, will we be in this room tonight, too?"

She jerked on his chain, pulling him slightly forward. "Naughty boy. Did I give you permission to speak?"

"No, Mistress."

"You've misbehaved too much tonight."

He looked down at his feet. "I'm sorry, Mistress."

Dr. Vickers cupped his chin. "I know you are, but you must be punished, sweetheart. I know you love this room, but Lex has plans for his sub here. I'm going to take you to the dungeon room to whip you into submission tonight."

The man smiled broadly, and I knew what he was feeling —excitement.

"Mia, Master Lex should be here any minute. I'm going to lock the door so no one can walk in on you. He's got the only other key to this room. Understand?"

I nodded, unable to call her by the name she'd requested I use here.

"Good." She and her sub walked to the door. She looked back at me. "Whatever you've been doing for Lex, keep it up. I've never seen him like this." Before I could ask her how he had changed since meeting me, Dr. Vickers closed the door. I heard the lock engage.

I was curious as to what I could be doing that would impact someone like Lex. He was a self-assured Dom. What could I do for him?

I took a seat at one of the student desks. It had the typical attached work surface that curved from the right directly in front of a person. I looked up at the white dry erase board behind the teacher's desk. I hadn't noticed the message written in blue marker when I'd entered.

Mia Weiss, see me after class. Professor Lex.

Seeing his name on the board supercharged my sexual anticipation. Still, the nagging voice in my mind had me worried. This needed to remain only fun and games or my heart wouldn't survive it.

Then Lex walked into the classroom. I was glad that tonight he wasn't wearing sunglasses or a leather mask. He didn't look my direction but headed straight for the teacher's desk. He didn't have to look at me. He didn't have to make a sound either. I would've known he was here. His presence filled the space in some intangible way that got my heart pounding. And the man could really fill out a suit. His tie was blue, which complimented his eyes. I'd seen him in very little, but something about the perfect cut of that suit was sexy as hell. He carried a brief-case, which he slammed so hard on the desktop it caused me to jump.

He turned his stare to me. "Miss Weiss."

It was starting. Everything feminine inside me softened with antici-pation. "Yes, Sir."

"You've done well up to this point in your studies."

"Thank you."

"Tonight is your final test. But..." His voice trailed off, causing a shiver to rip through me.

Of all the rooms he'd set up for me, this one worked even more quickly than the others to get me into the role. Clearly, it was closest to my life outside The Cell at the university, and he'd likely chosen it as my BDSM graduation. I knew I was in trouble. My body knew what to do, but my mind knew this might be the last time with Lex, causing a danger to my heart's well-being.

"I'm scared," I confessed.

He stepped up to me and cupped my chin. "Do you trust me, little sub?"

I should've stood up and left right then, but I couldn't. Train wreck or not, I did trust him. So I just nodded.

"Excellent. Time for you to earn some extra credit." Lex's confidence seemed to fill the room.

He'd been tough but very understanding with me, helping me discover more about myself than I'd been able to do my entire life. And the pleasure he'd given me...well, it was so overwhelming and incredible, I couldn't imagine living without it.

"Strip, sub."

I stopped, his words taking me off guard. "What?"

He leaned against the desk in front of mine. "Give your professor a show, understand?"

All my hesitation melted away. "Yes, Sir." I removed my shoes.

I felt that this moment was my chance. If I could turn him on and make him crazy with lust, maybe he would continue tutoring me. God, I hoped so. All I needed to do was tap into his animal instinct.

I'd been to a strip club when my cousin had his co-ed bachelor party a couple of years ago. The only women at the event were my cousins—Lea, Amy, Ella—and me and my sister, Misty. We got to see up close and personal how men acted when women stripped and swung from a pole. I wanted Lex to look at me the way those guys looked at those women that night.

I started unbuttoning my shirt, but my hands were shaking. Something was missing. I recalled the bachelor party. "Professor, is there any chance you have a way to play music in here?"

He chuckled, his warm approval seeping into my bones. "Setting the mood. Very good, Mia. You might just get an *A*."

Without a word, Lex walked back to the door to a panel that I'd not noticed when I'd come in. He opened it. I spotted a shelf with a keyboard and monitor hidden inside, and was once again impressed with The Cell's sophistication. Lex had created the most amazing club. No wonder its patrons came back again and again.

The song he selected sounded tribal, with its deep, resounding drum tracks. The rhythms were hypnotic and ethnic in feel, vibrating on my skin and raising my self-confidence.

"Work for you, little sub?"

"Oh, yes. Very much, Sir." I wanted him hot and panting, whatever it took.

I remembered the professionals at the strip club had taken their time, teasing the males into a frenzied state. By the time they were done, the guys had turned over their last dollars from their once fat billfolds.

I didn't want money from Lex, but I did want him crazed with desire for me.

Though several of the buttons on the oxford were undone, exposing the plaid bra, I left the shirt on, choosing to remove the scarf first. I slowed my pace, letting the music's thick beat set the rhythm for the roll of my hips. Lex's fixed gaze followed my fingers' moves, making me warm inside. Before him, I would've never even considered shedding my clothes for a man in such a way. But his adoration of my curves had turned me around over the past few nights. No longer did I see myself as overweight, but instead I felt beautiful.

Even though my palms were sweaty, I continued undressing, actually enjoying myself. Slowly and methodically, I unbuttoned the remaining buttons of my shirt until the plaid bra peeked out from the white cotton. Then I lowered the oxford off my shoulders, but pulled it across my chest, hiding the bra from his sight for a moment. For a split second, I turned away, as if shy to show him my chest. Then I faced him, pulling the two sides of the shirt apart to reveal my bra for only a moment. It was great being flirty with him. Back together and the bra could no longer be seen by him.

Lex looked like a hungry lion about to pounce, but he was too controlled for that. Or was he? Could I get him to leap from the desk and ravish me before I finished? Probably not, but I sure did want to try.

The drumbeat of the song coming from the hidden speakers

mirrored my pulse. Or was my pulse mirroring it? Slow. Deep. Rhythmic. I smiled at Lex and then dropped the shirt to the floor, covering up my bra with my arms to add to the temptation I was trying to create for him. I was thrilled that the move seemed to work magic on Lex, as I saw him lick his thick lips. My heart raced, and my body ignited with my own steamy desires. I was hot, so very hot. My pussy was aching, and I had only taken off my shirt. If I weren't careful, I would be the first to lose control, not Lex. But I didn't want that. So I focused, trying to think of more ways to heat him up.

I leaned back on the student desk, locking my hands behind my back so that my breasts jutted out more. In the sexiest tone I could muster, I whispered, "You think I'll pass, Professor?"

"You just might, little sub." He sent me a wicked wink. "With your hot body and sexy curves, you just might indeed."

His words nearly had me hyperventilating. I took almost ten minutes to remove my bra, trying to squeeze out every ounce of allure I could. Holding out for as long as possible, I covered my mounds with my hands, and I felt my nipples harden under my palms. Lex's breathing was heavy and loud, filling me up with pride on my job of my first striptease.

"Professor, I really need that A," I said, taking the role of naughty schoolgirl to heart.

Keeping hold of my chest, I stepped up to him.

His nostrils flared. "You're going to be trouble, aren't you?"

I looked into his blue orbs and moved to him until I could squeeze his left leg with my thighs. When I felt his hard-on through his trousers, I gulped. My pussy got even wetter. This was a fine line I was walking, but I wasn't about to hold back now.

"Is there something I can do for you, Sir? You want to fuck me? Just ask."

He lifted me up in his arms so fast that it startled me. There was a storm exploding on his face, and I had been the cause of it. My clit throbbed and my pussy clenched.

His nose touched mine, and he growled. "Little sub, I don't ask, I take."

I was shivering and panting. "Y-Yes, S-Sir."

I'd succeeded, but now, seeing him supercharged with lust, I was anxious that I might've overshot my mark and bit off more than I could chew.

Lex lowered me to the floor. "Time for your oral exam." His potent words were hitting me like a paddle to my ass, getting my pussy soaked. "On your knees, sub."

I obeyed and waited for his next instruction.

Unlike my crawling burlesque show, he was out of his clothes so fast I barely could catch my breath.

He grabbed my hair with one hand and cradled my chin with the other. "Open those gorgeous lips wide."

I obeyed, and he guided his thick dick down my throat like an intimate kiss. Down it went, until I could feel the tickle of his pubes on my nose. I reached out and cupped his balls, squeezing gently.

When his cock got into the deepest part of my throat, I slid my tongue out, slipping it along the underside of his dick.

"Feels so fucking good, sweetheart." Each lusty syllable came from deep in his chest.

He'd given me so much. I could never repay him, but I could give him the best I could deliver. I pressed my lips together around his dick, sucking so hard my cheeks hollowed out.

"Fuck. Fuck. Fuck."

Lex loved being in charge, holding the reins, but for this one moment, I needed to give him this. Tears streamed down my face, praying that tonight wouldn't be our last night together but wondering if it might. No matter what, I didn't want him to forget me. So I sucked on him with all I had, worshiping the man who had captured all of me.

"Take me, little sub. All of me. I want to drown you with my cum."

I could feel his cock jerk in my throat. He was close. I bobbed up and down his shaft and fondled his heavy balls, trembling from my own brazenness.

"Yes. Yes. Yes." Both his hands pressed at the back of my head. "Fuuck!"

I felt him send his cock to the very back of my throat, shooting his hot liquid into my mouth. I swallowed every drop.

When I felt his hands leave my hair, I sucked hard on him once again. He stiffened and then jerked on my hair, removing his cock from my greedy mouth.

"No, no, no, love. I'm the one that punishes, not you."

My cheeks burned. "Did I do something wrong, Sir?"

He kissed my forehead. "I guess you didn't know. So innocent. Amazing. Sweetheart, after a man comes, the nerves in the head of his dick are sensitive to the near painful for the first few moments. Any touch, and especially one from a sweet mouth like yours, is too much. Got it?"

I nodded. I hadn't known that. "I'm so sorry, Sir. I didn't mean to hurt you."

He smiled. "Good girl."

A blast of pride filled me up. To distract myself, I tugged at my skirt.

"That was great, sweetheart, but I have more planned for you tonight." He opened up the briefcase with the lid facing me so that I could not see in.

"What's next, Professor?"

He lifted me off the floor and sat me down on the desk. "Get on your stomach and find out."

I responded instantly, flipping over on the desktop.

"Such a greedy sub." Lex pulled down my skirt to my ankles.

When he massaged my ass, I moaned. It still had a bit of a sting left over from the previous nights, but he was working that out skill-fully. I felt him apply some lubricant to my backside entrance. He'd told me last night that he would fuck me in the ass tonight, and although I was anxious about my first anal experience, I was also very stirred up and hot for the prospect of it. Lex was a Dom, and it appeared to me that surrendering to him that way would speak to his nature to possess.

"I'm going to fill up your pretty ass with my cock." He tied my hands together over my head with his discarded tie and my ankles together with his belt. Then he used my scarf to blindfold me.

I was his trapped prey, his to do with however he pleased. I trusted him and I loved the feeling of complete helplessness. By taking away my other senses, he'd left me with no choice but to feel. To feel him.

"I'm going to pull you down a bit off the desk, so that you'll be on your tiptoes for me with your ass jutting out." And just as he'd promised, Lex lifted me up and moved me down the desk until I was in the position he wanted me in, bent over the desk.

He rubbed my back, ass, and legs with his calloused hands, making my skin tingle. My hair hung down around my face. With the restraints of his belt and tie, I was completely helpless. I couldn't move. The leather of his belt bit into my flesh, delivering a small hurt that electrified my skin. It was heaven.

His large palm crashed against my ass, bringing out the familiar hum of pain and pleasure. Smack. Smack. Smack.

"Feel the throb, Mia. My torments will make you more aware of your own body." I felt his fingers feather across my ass, causing my pussy to clench and moisten. "That's it. Nice."

I was panting, my lips releasing little gusts of my breath.

Smack. Smack. Smack.

"I'm going to fuck you until you can't see straight. God, your virgin ass is mine, little sub. It's all mine."

Smack. Smack. Smack.

I was getting deliciously dizzy. My mind let go of the past and the future and clung to the here and now.

Smack. Smack. Smack.

The heat in my ass sent hot sensations zipping through my body and into my pussy, which was completely soaked. Then I felt his finger pierce the tightness in my ass, going in deep. The pressure only added to my desire to be his, all his. I wanted him to take me any way he wanted. Another finger joined the other inside me, stretching my ass out, getting it ready for his massive cock.

"Have you used a vibrator, sub?"

"Yes, Sir."

"On your ass?"

"No, Sir. Not there. Honestly, I'm a little scared," I confessed.

"Baby, you're about to find out how much pleasure you can get that way." I heard him moving around the room, and moments later, I heard the hum of a vibrator as it kicked on. He slipped it between my ass's cheeks. "Take a deep breath. Good. Now, exhale and push out."

As I obeyed his instructions, he pushed the dick-shaped toy through my tightness. I gasped at the pain. Instantly, he pulled it out and the ache ended.

"This time, I want you to let the air out of your lungs in one big gush."

Again, I complied. As the last bit of oxygen escaped my lips, I could feel the tip of the vibrator pierce my ass, filling and stretching me out even more. The burn was intense, and Lex once more removed it from me. We repeated this several times, each breach of my ass easier than the last. I was no longer fighting against the toy in my ass. Now I was craving more.

"You're almost there, little sub. Once again."

I took as much air into my chest as I could and then blew it out. Lex sent the toy deep into my ass, sending tingling urges through my body. He began to thrust the vibrator in and out of my backside, torturously slow. Still on my tiptoes, he had me writhing from the perfect amount of discomfort.

He nearly pulled the vibrator completely out of my ass and held it there. I thought about shifting back into it, but didn't as Lex was in command, not me.

"Perfect. You're doing great, baby." Then he shoved it back into my ass, filling me up once again. The sting of the thing inside me still remained, but now alongside it was a fathomless want.

The thrusts of the toy were like incantations that spelled my body to red hot. In and out. Just as I'd become accustomed to one tempo, he would change the intensity, switching the vibrator's speed, and beginning his torture again. The medium setting seemed to work the best on me, and he clearly knew it, settling in on that speed for some time.

"You're on fire, Mia, and you're burning me up."

I writhed under the ministrations of the vibe, but I was still a little unsure. "I'm not certain I can take all your cock, Sir."

"Either use your safe word or don't." He paused as if waiting for me to utter it.

I didn't.

"Excellent. You floor me with your responses and how quickly you learn." His words were pleasure in and of themselves.

"Thank you, Sir."

"I'm going to fuck your perfect ass, little sub. I can't hold back any longer, and I know you're ready. Trust me. You'll love this."

Then I felt his hands on my ass cheeks parting my flesh. Though a bit frightened at what was to come, I'd never wanted anything more in my life than to have him plunge his dick deep into my ass. I could feel my pussy's wetness dripping along my legs. I hoped that once he had his dick in my ass, it would be his way of claiming me utterly.

I heard him rip open a condom package. "Take a deep breath and hold it in your lungs, Mia."

I obeyed, crazy to have him possess me. I couldn't give him my true virginity. I had tossed that aside, but this was my gift to Lex. He'd taught me so much. He'd brought me to myself.

"Let it out nice and slow."

I exhaled the air slowly, like a kettle on a stove, savoring the touch of the head of his cock against my tight entrance.

"Another."

Again I complied, totally submissive with him. The tip of his cock parted the first inch of my ass's depths, but it didn't pain me much, having been stretched by his fingers and the vibrator already.

"One more."

As I released the last breath, he shoved his cock into my virgin ass. The pain returned. His cock was larger than the vibrator by a lot. I clenched my jaw tight, and my hands curled into fists.

Lex didn't move another inch, but kept his dick deeply seated inside my ass. "Hang on, baby. Breathe."

Again, I obeyed him. It seemed that he knew my body better than I did because after inhaling and exhaling a few times, I was aroused beyond belief.

"There you go, little sub. You're there, aren't you?"

"Y-Yes, Sir." I panted.

Then he plunged in and out of me with abandon. I was his.

"Take me, Lex!" I screamed, as my nerve-endings blistered through me.

And for the first time, he seemed out of control, lost to his own passion. I've never been more lost and thrilled to be with someone than that moment with Lex.

"Fucking your ass, Mia. Your virgin ass. So fucking tight. Fuck. Fuck. Fuck."

Each syllable matched his strokes. In and out. Faster and faster. The drums still played from the hidden speakers, adding to the intensity of him fucking my ass.

His pounding continued, but I knew he was close, thankfully, as my own orgasm was about to turn me into a complete and utter livewire.

I clenched my ass as tight as I could around his dick.

"*Fuck!*" He yelled. I could feel his dick shoot its hot liquid.

He reached around me, applying pressure to my throbbing clit with his fingers. I'd been on the edge, but his stimulation on my bud of nerves worked to plummet me over the cliff.

"Yesssss...God...Oh...God...Yes. Yes. Yes."

I banged on the desk with my bound fists as a flood of sensations drowned me, and my womb convulsed again and again. Tears streamed down my face and my heart raced in my chest.

"That's my baby. Ride that orgasm." He began stroking my back, which fired off more tingles inside me.

We stayed in that very position, his dick in my ass and me bent over the desk, for what seemed an eternity until my climax slipped into a delicious hum.

Lex undid the belt around my ankles, and took off the tie from my wrists. Then he removed the scarf from my eyes. He flipped me around to face him, and I stared into the most beautiful blue eyes in the world.

"Mia, you get an A. You've passed the course."

"I did?" The words came out of my mouth in a languid stream. I felt so good. Complete.

Lex leaned in and kissed me deeply, passionately, sending his tongue past my lips and into my mouth.

More tears than I thought possible fell from my eyes. This man had taken me to places inside myself that I'd never known existed. He'd agreed to let me, the little grad student at the lecture, come to his club for a test. I'd passed. What now? Was this our last time together? Was this goodbye?

My heart was breaking in two as he ended our kiss.

"What's the matter, sweetheart?"

I couldn't find the courage to tell him my fears. The truth would kill me. "Lex, you say I passed. Will you let me interview you now?"

His eyebrows shot up. "That's all that's troubling you?"

"Yes," I lied. "What do you say?" If he agreed to an interview, then maybe there was still hope for me to be with him after all. Maybe.

"I don't like lying, Mia." By his tone, I knew he was not happy with me.

"Please, Lex. Ask Dr. Vickers. I need to work on my thesis."

"Okay. You'll get your interview. Tomorrow night. I have something I want to discuss with you, too."

I JUST CLOSED MY LAPTOP. All the questions for Lex are ready. But there's so much more I want to ask him.

I just can't let myself think tomorrow might be the end of my time with Lex. I'm in too deep. What a mess.

I love him. It's true.

My heart will never survive.

Jan 6th

※❀※

Diary, I'm still reeling about what happened during the interview with Lex. Let me start at the beginning.

As before, I was driven to the club in a limo. It was noon, so the place was closed. We were all alone at The Cell. He escorted me to his private office. The decor was quite sparse, with a modern edge. There was a desk, a table and chairs, open shelving, and a large whiteboard at the back wall.

"Sit there." He pointed to one of the chairs next to the table.

I nodded, and took a seat. Then I took out my laptop from my satchel and fired it up. I clicked on the interview doc I'd created for this moment.

Lex sat in the chair opposite mine. "You about ready to get this underway, Mia?"

"One more second, please." I finished entering the information about date, time, place, and Lex's full name. Then I looked up from my laptop and found him gazing at me with his lips curled up ever so slightly.

Clearly, he was amused by my nervousness, which instantly set me on edge.

Lex had told me last night that he wanted to talk to me about something immediately after my interview with him. I hadn't slept fearing what he wanted to discuss since leaving him last night. I knew from Viv and Dr. Vickers that he'd steamrolled through many women. Why in the hell did I think he would see me any differently? Feeling the hot blood in my face, I looked back at my screen with the questions I'd prepared for him. But these weren't the real questions I wanted to ask.

I took a deep breath. "Let's get started."

He looked utterly comfortable, and I was a wreck. "I'm ready. Give me your best shot."

"How old are you?" I sounded so idiotic.

"Going for the jugular, Mia?" He chuckled. "Thirty-two. My birthday is March twenty-ninth, if you want to give me a card or a present. I have something in mind I'd really enjoy from you."

My anxiety grew as my heart was ripping apart. "Are you going to take this seriously or not, Lex? You promised you would."

He smiled. "Go on."

Was this it? Were these my last moments with him? No more lessons. No more spankings. No more kisses. I tried to clear my thoughts but couldn't. He'd agreed to my interview. He wanted to hear logical questions from me. I recalled my blubbering performance on the day I'd met him in the lecture hall. If I wasn't going to see him again, I would at least like to think he would remember me as having a brain in my head.

I forced myself to speak calmly. "How long have you been practicing BDSM?"

His eyebrows shot up. Was he seeing into me? Reading my mind once again?

Lex moved his gaze to my fingers, which were trembling. "Ten years."

I placed my hands in my lap and stared back at my screen. I was having so much trouble thinking clearly. "So, you were twenty-two?"

"That's right."

I tried to imagine him at that age. He must've been quite the knockout on campus. But I wasn't sure if he'd gone to college. I felt completely muddled. Why couldn't I find the courage to ask him what

I really wanted to know? But did I even know how to ask? I didn't. So instead I continued with the questions I'd prepared. "What's the highest level of education you've completed, Lex?"

"I have my MBA. Does that surprise you?"

"Not really. You own a successful business and run it quite well from what I've seen."

His eyes narrowed. "You haven't seen everything, Mia."

No, of course not. I wasn't sure I had the courage to ask him to show me, no matter how badly I wanted it. I was on uneven ground with him.

Lex had all the advantages. "You have another question, or is the interview over?"

"Yes." I read off the next question from the survey on my laptop. "Are you single, married, divorced, or...um...in a committed relationship?"

I glanced back at him and found his stare fixed on me. Immediately, I looked back to my screen. Was there a woman in his past that had heard this all before? Jealousy sank its claws into my neck as I realized he might even have someone in his life right now. I might've just been a little plaything, the latest distraction for him. But trying to pry information out of such a man wasn't something I could risk.

"Umm. Let's table that one for now." My thoughts were jumbling up.

Lex's face darkened. "You really want to table that question, Mia?"

The hurt I felt was like a weight on my heart. Once we were done here, would I lose him for good? Probably. Tears stung the back of my eyes. I screamed inside my head to tell him how I felt, what I feared. But my screams went unheeded. I couldn't find my voice to tell him everything—or anything. Plus, I was afraid of what he might answer. Once again I looked at Lex, the man who had shown me so much and captured all of my heart.

My eyes brimmed with tears, but thankfully my voice remained steady. "Yes. Your personal life isn't important for my thesis."

His fists came down on the desk with a bang, taking me aback. "You're pissing me off."

"What? Why?" What had I done to get him so angry? I was angry, too. At least a part of me felt that way. I was also devastated and brokenhearted. And more. But that wasn't what he wanted to hear from me. I closed my laptop, hoping that would please him. "This better?"

"That's enough!" He came around the table and grabbed me by the shoulders. "I'm not putting up with this crap from you, sub. Do you understand?"

"N-Noo, Sir. I-I don't understand." Logic failed me. I'd done something wrong, but what? What could I say that he wanted to hear? "You don't want to do the interview? Then we won't do it, Lex."

He lifted me off the chair. He sat and pulled me over his lap. It took him less than a second to jerk my slacks down. "Fucking panties. Did I not text you today and tell you that you're not allowed to wear panties?"

I'd ignored his instructions, thinking there was no lesson or scene tonight with him. "Y-Yes, but—"

"Quiet." Lex didn't pull my panties down but instead ripped them to shreds with his bare hands. "You told me you trusted me, sub. Was that a lie?"

I'd never seen him so angry, and it frightened me. "I'm mixed up, Sir. I-I...things aren't..."

Whack! Whack! Whack!

The strike of his hand to my ass stung more than ever before. Unlike his previous spankings, this was real punishment.

"Did. You. Lie. To. Me?" Lex's indignant tone made me tremble.

My voice seemed to be paralyzed. The pain of his hand to my ass was unpleasant, but not even close to the pain I felt for displeasing him.

What could I say that would make him okay with me? I meant it when I said before that I trusted him, but now, I wasn't so sure. I wanted to, but this was clearly the final goodbye. That would leave me destroyed and lost. So I remained silent.

Whack! Whack! Whack! Whack! Whack!

Each smack brought my shame to the forefront of my mind. Tears streaked down my face. I wouldn't be able to sit comfortably for some time after this, but I didn't care. I deserved his wrath, all of it. He'd done nothing wrong. I was the one who'd led with my heart into our scenes together, not him. There'd been no promises from Lex. I'd let myself fall when he'd only done what he'd promised. He'd been my teacher, opening me up to my true self. Nothing more.

Whack! Whack! Whack!

He stopped spanking me and changed my punishment to painful pinches to my ass. I sobbed and sobbed. The truth...he deserved to hear all of it, no matter if he hated me for it.

The torture stopped abruptly.

Lex stood up, hoisting me to my feet. My slacks pooled around my ankles as I covered my face with my hands, unable to bear looking at him.

"Look at me, little sub." His voice was softer than earlier.

I obeyed, lowering my hands even though I knew my eyes were swollen and puffy.

He glared at me. "Answer me, not with what you want me to hear, but the actual truth. Now."

"Y-Yes, Sir." As more tears fell from my own eyes, I was finally clear about how I really felt about him, and I found the courage to say it. "I-I do trust you, Lex. I really do. But I was afraid to be open and honest with you today." Each syllable I uttered tore my heart apart, but holding back from him wasn't possible. Not now. Not after all he'd done for me. "You've helped me discover so much, and not just about my paper, but about me. I know I shouldn't want more from you, but God help me, I do. It's not fair to you. You made no promises to me. And it's my mistake that I've surrendered not just my body but also my mind, my dreams...m-my...very life. I-I'm...to blame...for..."

I couldn't go on and once again placed my face in my hands.

Lex lifted me up in his arms and squeezed me against his chest. I whimpered until no more tears fell.

"It's okay, sweetheart. I'm here."

I rubbed his chest and looked into his eyes, "For how long?"

"That's my girl." He pressed his forehead against mine and stared directly into my eyes. "Don't ever hold back from me again." He kissed me, and I gasped a little moan of surrender into his mouth. "You can always tell me what you're most afraid of. But hold back again and I'll have to punish you. Neither one of us wants that. Right?"

I shook my head.

"Now, let me tell you my truth. I went to my first club with some buddies my senior year in college. We all had a blast, but I found a life. It was like the blinders were off, and I knew myself for the first time."

"Lex, I—"

"Shh. Let me finish. I've been looking for you ever since that first night all those years ago. The moment I saw you at the lecture hall I felt the connection. Hell, more than that. Sure, I'm an experienced Dom and have trained my share of subs, but none of them are like you. This isn't some pain-trip for you like so many who use the life to repair some hurt from the past. Not a bad thing, I suppose, but not the kind of sub I want by my side. You're what I need, baby. I get you. Your very nature is to please and to surrender. Mine is to control. I can't deny that. And I fucking crave your total trust." He kissed me again, and my toes curled.

I loved how open he was being, but wasn't sure how anything could change. I might garner another night or two with him, but goodbye seemed to be inevitable. "Lex?"

"Quiet, little sub. I'm not done." He squeezed me again, and I melted against his hard frame. "Ask any real Dom what gets him off, and he'll tell you it's when he and his sub are in perfect sync, on every level. I know you, Mia. I *feel* you. We're on the same page, right?"

I nodded, recalling my time with him as my cop, as my dungeon master, and as my professor. Even now, I felt totally in tune with him. My heart filled up with happiness, but just as fast, it began to drain away. Did he want me only for play as a supposed super sub? Was that all I was to him? What if he couldn't commit, couldn't love? If not, I wouldn't be able to bear it.

"What about love, Lex?" I choked out. "Is that even possible with you?"

He was quiet for a moment, but I was no longer afraid. I was starting to believe. "I wasn't sure about that for such a long time. Now, I know what love is. I'm holding love in my arms. I want to share the rest of my life with you, Mia."

Tears rolled down my eyes and I touched his jaw. Joy exploded inside me like fireworks. He was my dream come to life, my *happily ever after*.

Once again, Lex kissed me. "I love you, my little sub."

"I love you, Master. I am yours."

Jan 7th

M ia, I finished reading your diary. I'm so proud of you for not only telling me about it, but also for trusting me enough to turn it over to me. Well, I've read every word, sweetheart, and I love you even more for it.

Don't worry about your thesis any more. I know some terrific people who will gladly sit down with you and answer any questions you have about the life. With my help, you're going to graduate in May, I promise.

You also mentioned an intruder fantasy you've used to help you masturbate in the past. Because I don't allow such thing now do, I?

But guess what, baby? I'm going to the club to get a room all set up just for you and me to give you that fantasy. I'll text you with instructions in about an hour. Be ready.

HI DIARY, this is Mia again.

Doesn't he know that he is my fantasy? I'm pretty sure he does. And lucky for me, I am his.

The End

LEA'S MÉNAGE DIARY

Feb 9th

Jerry just left.

Sobbing, he ended our relationship. Me? I couldn't even muster a single tear. Isn't that weird?

We've been together for six years and engaged for four. We'd actually set a wedding date last November. Even then, I didn't jump for joy. Instead, I actually dreaded June, the month of our pending nuptials. I'd felt so guilty about it but thought it was my own version of illogical cold feet. But deep down, I knew better.

Even though Jerry is a good man and will make some woman very happy one day, life for me with him would've been so dull, I would've ended up resenting him.

I'm actually glad he ended things between us because I know I never would have done it no matter how gray I thought our future would be together.

I guess at my very core, I'm a coward.

I would've rather kept letting the clock tick away until I was in a white gown headed down the aisle than confront him. I don't deal well with conflict. I turn into a frozen icicle whenever things get tough. I hate that about myself, but I just can't help it. There are two kinds of people in the world: the takers and the givers. I fall into the later category, God help me.

But what am I to do now? I haven't been in the dating scene in years. Being twenty-six and size sixteen, I can't imagine I'm going to see a bunch of prospects lining up for a chance to date me.

Probably not a good idea to be eating this chocolate ice cream, but damn it, I just got dumped.

I can start working on getting into my dating weight tomorrow.

Feb 10th

My cousin Mia came over this afternoon. Sometimes I wonder if she's psychic. She always shows up whenever I need someone to talk to.

She looks amazing. I was still in my pajamas, still numb, and still trying to figure out what I want to do with the rest of my life.

I've never seen her happier. She's got a man in her life that clearly is responsible for her turnaround.

Last time I saw Mia, she was a mess, worrying about her master's thesis and a ton of other things. She was single and hating it. Now, she and her guy have moved in together. I'm thrilled for her.

Mia is coming back to get me tonight. She's taking me to her boyfriend's club, The Cell. I've heard about it before. Apparently, it's a club that caters to a very wealthy clientele who like their kink served up in such a way that their Versace bags and Manolo shoes don't seem out of place. Damn, what was I thinking when I said "yes" to Mia? Obviously I wasn't thinking at all. I am curious, though. Very.

My past sex life with Jerry was blah at best. I've never had an orgasm. Even masturbating, I just can't seem to get there. I'd thought about asking him to mix it up in the bedroom with some play and experimentation, but never did. I knew how he would feel about it.

Jerry's life has always been and always will be about numbers. That's why he is in the perfect job. He's an actuary for a major insurance company.

I'm looking in my closet for something that will not be hideous to wear tonight, which is sending me into a complete funk. Even though I'm only supposed to get a tour of the club with Mia and Lex, I still want to look good. Is that even possible with the crap I have? Probably not.

Maybe I should call Mia and cancel.

~

I CALLED MIA. Of course, she wasn't about to let me back out of it. When I told her I didn't have anything appropriate to wear, she came up with an apparent solution. "I've got the answer, Lea. I'll text you an address. Meet me there in twenty minutes. Viv can fix you up."

And, per normal, I gave in to her demand. Why don't I have any backbone? I'm sitting in my car outside this store that caters to the kinky set, waiting for Mia and completely dreading trying on clothes.

~

I AM TOTALLY SPENT and still vibrating from what happened tonight at The Cell. Wait—I want to get everything down so I won't forget it.

Let me go back to the outfit that Mia and the store's owner, Vivian, picked for me to wear. I have avoided anything white for years, preferring dark colors. But when I looked at myself in the full-length mirror in the white gown they'd chosen, I was actually pleased with my reflection, which almost reminded me of a fairy-tale princess.

Mia's eyes were wide with apparent awe. "You look amazing, Lea. Don't you agree, Viv?"

"I certainly do agree," she stated. Vivian looked to be in her late twenties. Her dark bob haircut was stunning, as was the ink on both her arms. She seemed like a woman who could hold her own just about anywhere.

"Compared to who?" I asked, pointing at Mia in her black vinyl teddy. "I'm betting the second your man gets an eyeful of you, he's going to cancel my tour and take you back home for some hot sex."

Mia laughed. "Actually, he's set up a scene for us at midnight."

"What's a scene?" I asked, realizing I was headed into a whole new realm I knew little about.

"Lex worked in the movie industry for a brief stint before he opened his club. He loves creating new realms for his customers. There are lots of rooms that are set to bend reality for the participants. We're going to have fun in the Villain and Superhero room tonight. We were a hit when he played the criminal and bested me. I wore a red cape and everything. Tonight, I get to be the villain, but he's still going to win. He always does." Her lips curled up into a sweet grin.

"What do you mean 'you were a hit' in that room?" I felt my cheeks get hot, thinking about Mia being so wild and open. She definitely had changed, and how. "People can watch?"

Mia nodded.

Viv laughed. "Lea, you're going to be quite the hit tonight yourself."

I didn't believe her, but smiled broadly. "No way. Mia. This is only a tour, right?"

My cousin giggled, but didn't answer. She'd always been a bit of a jokester, even when we were younger. I was certain she was just teasing me. There was no way I would ever be intimate with a guy tonight, let alone in front of people.

Lex had sent a limo for Mia and me. I was wringing my hands the entire drive, wishing I had figured a way out of this whole evening. I would've much rather been watching the movie with Leonardo and Kate that never failed to make me cry than headed off to The Cell.

When the limo stopped by the side door entrance, my heart was pounding hard in my chest.

Mia got out of the vehicle like a giddy schoolgirl. "There he is." She pointed to a very handsome man standing to the side of the door. He wore a jacket, jeans, and boots. She'd told me he'd worked in the movie industry, but I had no idea that he was leading-man material. He was no pretty boy, but had a manly, rugged look that could've landed him many lucrative roles. No wonder she was so gone on Lex.

He was quite the sexy hunk. "Come on, Lea. I can't wait for you to meet my guy."

She didn't wait for me, but actually ran into his arms.

Lex hoisted her up and spun her around. "How's my little sub tonight?"

"I'm really excited to show you off to my cousin."

He lowered her down to her feet and extended his large hand to me. "You must be Lea."

"In the flesh. Nice to meet you, Lex."

He reached out, and his large hand engulfed mine, making me feel tiny. "Same here. Mia's told me a lot about you."

I wondered how much she'd shared with him. "She's told me quite a bit about you, too. You're the reason for the permanent smile on her face, I assume."

He placed his arm around Mia. "She's done the same for me, Lea, and more."

Mia leaned into him, and I could clearly see the utter joy and happiness on her face. These two were completely in love, not the lukewarm, lackluster fondness I'd felt with Jerry, but the head-over-hells, heart racing, can't-live-without-you, wild and crazy kind of love. My own heart ached for that, but I doubted I could ever feel such a thing with anyone. Hell, I had trouble feeling anything at all. Whenever I did reach into my emotions, they were always muddled and hard to explain. Often, I felt cut off from my own self.

"Shall I show you what I've set up for you, Lea?"

Set up? He must be talking about the tour. I choked out, "Yes. I'm ready. Lead on."

We walked into the reception area.

"Give me a consent form," Lex said to the woman sitting behind the desk. She nodded and pushed over a pen and some papers attached to a clipboard. He wrote on the last page and then handed it to me. "Lea, read this and sign it for me please."

Though he'd said "please," it didn't sound like a request but more of a command. I found his demeanor odd, but somehow comforting. Still, I wondered what kind of place required a person to have to sign release forms. It wasn't like I was going to be bungee jumping tonight. Or was I?

I skimmed the contents, which caused my hands to shake. Along with the legalese of the release, it had some information on what a new client could expect. There were some Dos and Don'ts, and more. Being a single woman here apparently did have its privileges. No one was allowed to approach me without the permission of the Dom acting as my guide in the club. Lex had put his name in that field. Strangely, I felt relieved to sign the thing.

After I signed my name and dated it, I gave it back to Lex.

He looked it over and nodded. "Perfect."

"Where are we going, Master?" Mia asked.

I was shocked to hear her call him that, but in an odd way, it did seem appropriate.

"To one of the training rooms. Reed and Kane are waiting for Lea."

"What?" I squeaked out.

Lex grinned. "Not a what, Lea, but a couple of whos."

I frowned. "*Who* then?"

"You'll be perfectly fine with the twins," Mia chimed in.

My cheeks burned hot. I wasn't ready to meet any new men, but it was clear that Mia had put Lex up to finding me a date. Apparently, I was being given a choice between two. Or was I? Did they mean for me to jump into this hot pool with both feet and into my first ménage?

My old doubts almost shoved aside my timid nature and allowed me to voice my concerns—*almost*.

Lex folded the papers and stuffed them into his jacket, handing the clipboard back to the receptionist. "Let's get on with your tour, little lady." He put his left arm around Mia and his right arm around me.

I walked beside Lex and Mia with my lips pressed firmly together, shaking like a leaf but also so very curious. My emotions, normally buried deep in my psyche, were clear and powerful, jumping with a crosswise mix of cautious anxiety and wicked eagerness.

We went down several hallways and got a glimpse of the "scenes" Mia had informed me about earlier. The very atmosphere of The Cell was thick with sexuality, and its patrons were both beautiful and dangerous looking. I felt totally out of place, and my apprehension grew.

We came to a hallway with only four doors but no windows looking into the rooms. They were marked with the letters "A," "B," "C," and "D." Lex led us to the door with the letter "C" on it.

He knocked, and oddly, I felt a tingle spread through me. I wondered why I was reacting this way.

The door opened, and two of the sexiest men I'd ever seen in my life stood there.

The one with the long, dark hair smiled, causing me to go weak in the knees. "You must be, Lea." He extended his hand for me to take. I did. He squeezed my hand, and a hot jolt shot up my arm from where we touched. "I'm Reed. Welcome."

He wore a tight, black sleeveless T-shirt that accentuated the thick muscles it covered. His biceps bulged and were decorated with gorgeous ink. The left tat was an intricate design that looked tribal to me. The right tat was of a formidable-looking dagger that was softened a bit by the wings it was on top of. His eyes were light brown and surrounded by the thickest lashes I'd ever seen on any man.

"Are you going to hold hands all night or are we going to get started on the training?" His twin asked. Except for his shaved head and different tats, the two Doms were identical.

"S-sorry...I-I'm new to this," I stuttered, jerking my hand back.

"Stop it, Kane. Don't scare the girl away," Reed interjected.

Kane shrugged and then reached out and cupped my chin, causing my belly to flip-flop. "I don't think she'll bolt, bro. I can see excitement in her eyes."

I was about to voice my denial when a man came up behind us. This guy was taller than the other three by a fraction of an inch. His chin had one of those sexy indentions. I wondered where the average-looking male members of The Cell were milling. I sure hadn't seen any.

"Boss, we have a problem," the man told Lex.

Mia's boyfriend frowned. "What's the problem, Trip?"

"Steve didn't show up for the new member's seminar. We've got six couples who have been waiting on him for twenty minutes."

"Fuck." Lex shook his head. "If Steve shows up, fire him on the spot."

"Sure thing, but what do we do about the new members?" the man named Trip asked. "I've got Kevin talking to them right now, but he's got to leave to take care of his baby."

Lex rubbed his chin. "Right. His wife is a nurse who works nights. Damn. I set up a scene for Mia and me that I was looking forward to." He turned to Mia, who was frowning. "Sorry, pet. I guess we'll have to wait on—"

"Hold on, Lex." Kane let go of my chin. "I'll do the seminar. You and your sub deserve a night together. You've been working way too hard. Besides, Reed can handle this little morsel just fine for her first lesson."

Trip smiled. "That would be great, buddy."

"Thanks, Kane." Lex pulled Mia in tight and kissed her cheek. "We've been looking forward to this for a while."

"It's nothing, Lex. Happy to do it." Kane turned back to me. "You're in good hands, Lea."

I wondered if he was jumping at the chance to leave to avoid spending time with me. With his looks, he could easily bag more than his share of model types, and the same was true for Reed. I didn't want to be some kind of task to fulfill for Reed just because his boss asked it.

I turned to Lex and Mia. "I think I'm done here. I appreciate what you are trying to do for me, but I'm fine. People get unengaged all the time. I'll head home and let you two have your fun—"

"Lea," Reed said softly, making my insides melt. "Stay."

I looked in his piercing eyes and could not refuse him. "Okay. If you're sure you don't mind."

He stroked my hair, and heat shot through me. "My pleasure, doll."

"Lead the way to the new members, Trip." Kane followed after the man and was gone.

"Here's her info, Reed." Lex handed him my paperwork. "Cross off my name and put your name down for her guide."

"This ain't my first rodeo, boss. She's in good hands."

"I know. That's why I chose you guys."

"You sure you're going to be okay, Lea?" Mia asked.

I wasn't, but lied, "I'm fine. Go. Have fun with Lex."

After they left, Reed grabbed my hand and pulled me into the room. I hadn't looked past him and his brother to what the space looked like earlier, but now I did. It was about twenty by twenty feet and had tables along two sides. On the tables were paddles, whips, handcuffs, dildos and more, clearly identifying what the room was meant for.

I pointed to the three odd-looking contraptions in the room. "What are those?"

He grinned. "Eager? I like eager. That one is a St. Andrews Cross. The one over there is a bondage chair. The one in the middle is what I'm going to start you out on. It's an excellent spanking horse. Kane designed it himself."

The thing was black and looked similar to something you might see at a gym, with lots of levers to adjust the height and the tilt of the person on it. There were extensions for one's arms and legs that also adjusted to a variety of positions.

Maybe I should've run for the exit, but I didn't. In the oddest way, I felt comfortable in the room and more than a little excited.

Reed led me to the spanking horse. "Sit."

Enjoying his commanding tone, I complied. He walked over to one of the tables and produced a pen. He scribbled on the paperwork and brought it and the pen back to the spanking horse.

He handed both to me. "Put your initials next to my name and date it."

"You guys are quite official with this stuff, aren't you?"

"Yes. It's important that everyone knows what they are agreeing to, Lea. The Cell does not tolerate infractions to its rules."

"What exactly am I agreeing to, Reed?" Another wave of anxiety swept over me.

"You're putting me in charge."

"Of me?" I wasn't sure how I felt about that.

He smiled. "Yes, of you. But that doesn't mean I can do anything I want with you."

I looked over at the table of paddles and whips. This wasn't what

I'd expected to find when Mia invited me to The Cell, and yet I felt drawn to experience more. I needed to get a grip on myself. This wasn't something I'd ever done before. "I don't understand. This is all too much. I thought I was only coming here tonight to get a tour, not a lesson."

"If that's what you would like, I can give you a tour and then put you in a cab." Reed touched my cheek with one hand and grabbed a fistful of my hair with the other. I felt the slightest tug, which made me tingle. "Is that what you really want, sweetheart?"

I closed my eyes. Though my nerves were totally on edge, my curiosity urged me on. Besides, when would I ever have another chance to be instructed by someone as sexy as Reed? I shook my head. "No. I want the lesson. I'm scared, but I want to try."

"That's all I'm asking, pet. Now, open your eyes and sign the paper."

I instantly obeyed.

Reed took the pen and paper back. He scanned the pages and nodded. Then he folded it up and placed it in his front pocket.

"Let's get started, trainee." Reed sat down beside me on the horse. He caressed my neck and face with his fingertips, raising my temperature several notches. "The world you've just entered is about control and submission. A Dom uses control to help the submissive reach the very limits they've set for themselves and to push past them. The key component is trust, but that deepens with experience and time. Trust is the gift that both Dom and submissive crave. It unifies them together in the most intimate way."

"It sounds so beautiful when you describe it," I confessed.

"Kitten, it is beautiful." He kissed me with a fervency that made my toes curl and my pussy ache. With such skill that I felt dizzy, he continued kissing me like no man had ever done before. As his tongue swept into my mouth, I felt new sensations sparking to life inside me.

Just as suddenly as he'd begun our kiss, he ended it. "The relationship of Dom and sub is about controlling the mind. The Dom must be utterly in tune to the submissive. He reads her body's signs so that he knows where her head is and can administer exactly what she needs to surrender fully."

The more he told me about what Doms and submissives did, the more I wanted to sample it. Not just from anyone, but from him.

"First things first. You need a safe word."

"I don't know what you mean."

He smiled broadly and kissed my cheek. "So very sweet and fresh. Okay. Listen up, Lea. You and I haven't explored trust yet, right?"

I nodded, hanging on every one of his words.

"I'm very well trained as a Dom, but you don't know that yet. It's clear to me that your nature is to submit, but I don't know your limits, either hard or soft."

Something about his voice was getting me hotter and hotter. I needed to focus on his lesson. "What's the difference between hard and soft?"

"A hard limit is something you feel very strongly about and can't see yourself surrendering to no matter what. Do you have any phobias?"

"Only spiders."

"Noted. I've never used spiders in scenes, so not a problem." He went on, sounding like a tutor with a pupil. "I'm certain you have other hard limits you don't even know you have yet. I'll deal with that if it happens."

My jaw dropped. "Tonight?"

"Close your mouth, Lea. Listen and learn."

I heeded his instruction, pressing my lips together.

He winked at me. "Soft limits actually are very useful in a scene. They're the things you haven't tried successfully or at all but honestly are intriguing to you."

"Like what, Reed?"

"For you? Since this is your first venture into BDSM, anything." His voice lowered to a deeper octave, reaching into me and vibrating my skin. "Have you ever had your ass paddled before?"

"No." I felt a tingle in my pussy at the thought of the sex-on-a-stick man spanking my bottom.

Reed smiled. "But I can see by the look on your face that you find it appealing, though you're not sure what to expect. Right?"

I gulped, realizing how easily he could see into me. "Yes."

"Soft limits with the right Dom and under the right circumstances are opportunities to explore for both the Dominant and submissive. Once trust is found in a certain activity—"

"Like spanking," I interjected.

He shook his head and smiled. "You are such an antsy trainee, Lea. Yes, like spanking. With trust firmly in place, the soft limit is changed into an activity of play and pleasure to enjoy between the Dom and his sub."

"Sounds amazing to me," I confided.

Reed tenderly touched my cheek with his fingertips. "I think I may have found my perfect student in you, Lea."

I couldn't help but smile.

Though Reed never dropped his gaze from my eyes, he didn't speak again for what seemed to me to be several minutes. Suddenly, he removed his hand from my face and continued. "A soft limit is a place you need me to pause for a moment. You might even want me to change things up a bit in how I'm proceeding."

"How do I do that?"

"By using safe words. They are words or phrases that are agreed upon by both the Dom and the sub to alter or stop a scene. I've found that 'red,' 'yellow,' and 'green' work best as safe words for trainees. You can call them out whenever you feel the need. Think of a traffic light, Lea. Red tells the driver to hit the brakes. Yellow is use caution to proceed. Green is—"

"Go," I interrupted, and immediately regretted it. "Sorry, Reed."

"Not a problem, pet. I like your excitement. You're right. Green is go. Are you in agreement to use the colors as our safe words?"

I loved when he said "our" and nodded.

"Good. Truthfully, pet, after we do a few scenes together, you won't need any safe words. I'll be in tune to your needs more than you. Let me show you a few paddles." He stood.

Anxiety and excitement thickened in my mind. "Are you planning on spanking me, Reed?"

His eyebrows shot up. "Interesting idea, trainee, though my first thought was to just give you some verbal instructions for this lesson. But you're wanting to take the fast track, aren't you?" Before I could answer, he continued in a commanding tone. "Since we're going to scene together, no more calling me 'Reed.' You will address me as 'Sir' or 'Master Reed,' understand?"

I choked out, "Yes, Sir."

"There you go. Better. On your feet, trainee."

Believing things were about to take a hot, lusty turn, a flash of heat thawed my insides as I left the spanking horse.

"I am going to undress you," he stated bluntly.

Blood filled my cheeks from the embarrassment. What would he think of my body? A flash to resist and end the lesson with the word he'd given me came and went. I just didn't have the will to stop him, no matter how disconcerting it was going to be for me to be naked in front of him.

He made me turn around and pulled my dress over my head. He draped it neatly over the bondage chair.

It seemed as if he was taking his time with me for my benefit, making sure I was, if not relaxed, at least willing to continue in the path he'd laid out before me. After he removed my clothing, save my panties and bra, he stepped back and scanned my body.

All at once, I *saw* him—really saw him. What the hell was I thinking?

Reed was male perfection, muscled in all the right places. Under his Dom demeanor was a kind man with a really big heart. Me? I was female, but perfection...? No way.

Instinctively, I wrapped my arms around my bra, the only thing covering my breasts at the moment. "Sir, I'm really getting nervous about this."

Smiling, Reed got right in front of me. "I know, pet. I know." He grabbed my wrists and lowered them to my sides. "All part of it." He paused, and then said, "Fuck, you are gorgeous."

I shook my head, unable to believe him.

"Sub, you calling me a liar?" His threatening tone made me catch my breath.

"No, Sir."

"That's a good thing." He cupped my breasts through my bra, sending a shiver from where his hands touched down to my pussy. "Don't forget your safe words. Use them if you must. You will not be punished for uttering them." He removed my bra, and my cheeks burned hot. I couldn't believe I was going through with this, allowing a man I just met to see my breasts, but I couldn't find it in me to end this. With Reed's confidence and manliness, all I could latch onto inside me was desire—and submission. "They are just another set of tools for us to explore with."

I was enflamed with want. "Yes, Sir."

He pinched my nipples, making them hard and throbbing madly. "Are you on any medication, trainee?"

Shaking my head, I wondered why he would ask such a question.

"Good." He removed his hands off my chest, and I instantly missed them. "Some prescription drugs can change the level of a sub's pain threshold. Not a problem for you and me since you're not on any. Same with menstruating. Are you?"

I was flustered at the crude question but couldn't help but answer him. "No, Sir."

"We are in agreement about this scene's protocol. I will honor your safe words. When I ask you your state, you will tell me the color you most feel at that moment, but you don't have to wait for me to ask, trainee. You may call them out at any time without my permission. Understand?"

I pursed my lips, growing impatient to feel him touch me again. "Yes, Sir."

"My little trainee is getting restless, aren't you?"

I nodded, chewing on my lip.

"Too bad. You're not in charge here. I am." The timbre in his voice let me know he meant it. "Yellow doesn't mean a full-on stop, trainee, but it will give us a chance to pause and discuss what you're feeling. There is no shame in you calling out 'red' either. You understand me?"

Something about Reed's thorough instructions was getting to me. "I do, Sir."

"I swear I will not cross your hard limits, trainee. I will respect you and will earn your trust. Let's get into our scene. Face down on the spanking horse, trainee."

My heart thudded in my chest, and my palms dampened. "Now?" I asked.

He answered, "Right now."

I flipped around as he'd instructed.

"We're going to do this without restraints, tonight. I want to save something for your next lesson."

Though I was already feeling more than a little trust for Reed, I was glad he wasn't going to tie me down. Still, the idea did sound appealing in a way. That he thought there would be a "next lesson" thrilled me.

"Very good, trainee." I felt his hand go up and down my back, causing my skin to tingle. "Comfortable?"

"Yes, Sir."

"You won't be for long." Reed jerked my panties down to my ankles, kindling fiery sensitivity in my body. "Not long at all." Then he slapped my ass with his open hand, delivering a delicious sting to my flesh.

My pussy moistened, and my clit began to throb.

From the corner of my eyes, I could see him walking over to one of the tables. He selected what looked to me like a large ping-pong paddle, though it was black in color, not the blue or green I'd seen on others of its ilk.

Reed came back to the spanking bench. He put the paddle in front of my eyes. "See this?"

"Yes, Sir."

"This is going to give you a lesson you won't forget, trainee. Pleasure is what you crave, and when you please me, that's what I'll give you." As if to give an example of what he'd just told me, I felt him caress my ass with his free hand. "What state are you in?"

I answered "Green, Sir, but I do have a question."

"Ask."

"Umm..." Suddenly, I was tongue-tied and so very nervous.

A slap to my ass jolted me back. "I said 'ask.' Now."

I blurted out, "Do you plan on having sex with me?"

"I'd love to, trainee. God, would I love to. But this is your first lesson. No intercourse tonight. This time is only for training, understand?"

A mix of relief and disappointment rolled through me. "I do, Sir. Thank you."

"That doesn't mean you won't orgasm, trainee. If I do my job correctly, you definitely will climax. This time is for your pleasure only."

The promise of such release had me melting inside with need and heat.

"Time to spank that beautiful ass of yours, Lea."

I was vibrating like a leaf dancing on the heat waves of a forest fire.

Whack! The slap of the paddle to my left ass cheek stung. Tears welled up in my eyes, but I didn't cry out.

"What state, pet?"

"Green, Sir. I'm green."

"Excellent. Remember our agreement. Use your safe words."

"Yes, Sir."

Whack! Whack!

I moaned and thrashed on the spanking bench. Each strike of his paddle hit a different spot on my ass. My body was sizzling with new sensations.

"Trainee, what do you think about when you masturbate?" Reed asked firmly.

"I-I'm not sure what to say. I have many fantasies." I wished I could take back that admission. He must've thought I was a slut now.

"Of course you do, pet. Everyone does." He stroked my thighs with his free hand and the paddle. "What's your favorite fantasy? Your go-to, never-fails-to-get-you-off fantasy?"

An image of his brother floated in the back of my mind. "I'm not sure."

Whack! This strike was harder than the earlier ones and released the tears from my eyes.

"No lying. Tell me, trainee."

"Multiple partners, Sir."

Again, the caresses returned. "Enlighten me. Tell me about your fantasy."

I'm not sure if it was because I didn't want to disappoint him again, or if I already was beginning to trust him with my secrets, but I did tell him. "This is only a fantasy, Sir."

"Stop stalling, trainee. I know what it is. Remember, I asked the question. Tell me."

"Yes, Sir. I imagine myself between two men."

As though there was nothing odd about the concept, he said, "Threesome. Nice. Is one of your dream men fucking your pussy and the other your ass?"

"Yes, Sir." I was getting even wetter from his lusty inquiry and squirmed on the spanking horse.

"Your state, trainee?"

Without hesitation, I said, "Green."

"I want you to imagine your two men, trainee. They are here, and one of them is going to spank you, not for any disobedience, but to quiet your thoughts and get you into a state where you can really enjoy pleasure. Understand?"

"Some," I admitted.

"Let me see if I can explain better what I'm attempting. You'll hear people talk about 'subspace' from time to time here at The Cell. That's what I'm going to try to send you into now, trainee. It may or may not work since this is your first time."

"What is 'subspace,' Sir?" I asked timidly.

"Kind of like a trance for the sub. I want you to use your masturbation fantasy while I paddle your pretty, little ass, understand?"

I nodded, feeling my excitement grow.

"Good. Bring it up into your thoughts, trainee."

Instantly, I saw my familiar guys walk into my bedroom. During my personal playtime, I'd never been able to see their faces clearly, but now I could. One looked exactly like Reed, and the other his brother, Kane.

"All set?" he asked.

"Yes, Sir."

Whack! Whack! Whack!

In my mind, the visions of Reed and Kane were slapping my ass alternately with the paddles they held in their hands. I went higher and higher, to new plateaus filled with powerful sensations. Reveling in the fantasy Reed had instructed me to focus on, I closed my eyes tight as the spanking continued.

Whack! Whack! Whack!

The last strike to my ass from Reed's paddle quieted my mind to a whisper.

"I'm going to spank you with my open hand, pet." The lusty pitch of Reed's voice worked to send me into a hot craze. "I want to feel your skin on my hand."

Slap! Slap! Slap! Slap!

My pussy was soaked, and my clit was aching. I was thrashing on the spanking horse. Nothing had ever gotten me so close to savory madness before as did Reed spanking my ass.

Suddenly, I felt Reed's hand between my legs, threading through my swollen folds. I was awash with want.

"You did great, pet." His praise meant so much to me. "Time for your reward."

His fingertips touched me in all the right places, driving me to the brink of mania. I felt him part my pussy lips with them and press on my clit with his thumb. When his hot breath skated across my ass, I thought I would die from the unending desire inside me.

"Come for me, little trainee." I felt his lips on my ass, giving me the sweetest kiss I'd ever had in my life. Then he commanded, "Now. Come now."

Everything inside me erupted, and not a cell in my body could stay still. I screamed and screamed as my climax rocked me with a million sensations, some hot, others electric, but all overwhelming. I felt the spasms in my pussy and screamed again.

"Fuck, Lea. You are so very hot."

My tears flooded the spanking horse, and I panted as another orgasmic tremor scorched through me. Unable to stop shaking, I just closed my eyes and rode out wave after wave of the release he'd given me. I'd never felt more alive in my life or more connected to anyone than Reed. Discovering the frenzy that had always been buried deep inside me had only come about because of him, my teacher, my Dom.

"This is an ointment that will take some of the sting away, Lea." He applied the cream to my ass, and it felt amazing.

I wanted to thank him, to tell him how grateful I was, but I couldn't utter a single word yet with my body still reeling from my climax.

When he pulled up my panties from my ankles, I didn't say the words of gratefulness that I'd planned. How could I? Clearly, Reed had trained many women. I was just another first timer in his long line of students. When I finally did speak, I said, "Are we done, Sir?"

"For tonight, yes, trainee. We're done. How are you doing?"

I sighed, wondering what it would've been like to feel him inside my body. "I'm great, Sir."

"You are great, Lea. The scene is over now. You can call me by my name."

Unable to hold back my wholehearted appreciation, I blurted, "Thank you, Reed. Thank you very much."

"You're welcome, sweetheart. Let me help you up." Reed guided me to a sitting position.

I was woozy, but leaning into his muscled frame steadied me. "What's next?"

"I'm going to dress you," he stated. After I was back in my clothes, I started to stand but he placed his hand on my shoulder. "The scene is over but not the lesson, Lea."

"Oh really?" I was hoping for more kisses and caresses from him.

"Yes, really."

"So, what now?" I asked.

"Now, we're going to talk about what you can expect for tomorrow's training session."

Feb 11th

I was a bundle of nerves when I arrived at The Cell tonight.

Trip, the Dom who'd needed Kane to give the new member's seminar the night before, sat at the desk. He was on the phone giving someone directions to the club. I'd been so nervous at the time that I hadn't really taken full survey of the man. He had dark, thick hair. His eyes were deep green and sparkled in the light of the reception area. Both his upper arms were decorated with tats that looked like barbed wire circling his biceps. There was his dimpled chin that I had actually noticed last night. Rugged and handsome, he exuded a male confidence that could easily ensnare almost any unsuspecting female.

But I wasn't here for him. I was here for another training session with Reed.

When Trip hung up the phone, he brazenly looked me up and down. When his eyes met mine, he asked, "Have we met?"

"I'm Mia's cousin, Lea. I was here last night." I felt my insides melting at his unblinking gaze.

He finally looked down at the sign-in book at his fingertips.

"I'm here for Reed," I choked out. "He's going to train me."

His lips curled up at the corners. "I remember you. My name is Trip, and I wouldn't mind taking my turn with you, Lea."

I gulped and felt my cheeks burn. "I remember your name, too. My instructor is Reed, though."

He nodded, his smile broadening. "Take a seat, trainee."

Sitting on the sofa in the reception area, I wrung my hands together. Of course I was nervous since I didn't have Mia or Lex with me.

Keeping my stress in check, I recalled last night how Reed had opened me up to new and wonderful possibilities. I'd slept like a baby, but the moment I'd awoke this morning, excitement had taken hold of me. I couldn't wait for more from him. More training. That's what I craved.

"Hello, Lea."

I turned and saw someone who looked identical to Reed, save one thing. This sexy man didn't have Reed's long, dark hair. In fact, he didn't have any hair at all. His head was shaved, which normally wouldn't have been something I was attracted to, but on him it looked yummy.

"You're Reed's twin. Kane, right?"

He nodded.

I extended my hand, and he clasped it in his. "Nice to meet you, Kane."

"I've got a private room all set up for us."

For us? My jaw dropped. Reed wasn't going to train me tonight? He'd seemed okay with me last night. Maybe he'd only worked with me as a favor to Lex. "I thought Reed was going to continue my instruction?"

"His dog got hit by a car, and he had to take him to the vet."

I wasn't expecting to hear that. "Oh my God. Is the dog okay?"

Kane smiled. "Beast has more lives than a cat. I'm betting he'll live."

"Beast? That's an odd name for a dog. What kind is it?"

He dropped my hand and turned away from me. "A complete mutt. I think he's a mix between a German shepherd, Doberman, and Lab. Ugly creature, but Reed loves him. I just tolerate him."

His words didn't match the softness I heard in his voice. "I can tell by your tone that you're fond of the dog too, despite what you're actually saying about him."

Kane's eyebrows shot up. "I see I'm going to have my hands full with you tonight. Let's get started."

"Wait a second. I'm okay to come back tomorrow when Reed is available."

He frowned. "You definitely need training."

I'd obviously broken some kind of protocol. I wasn't sure what, though I'd read a bunch on the topic from the website Mia had suggested to me when we'd had lunch today. "Kane, I'm not trying to piss you off or anything. I just would be more relaxed—"

"Quiet." His tone was low, where only I could hear him, but still very threatening. "Not another word until we get into the room. If you want to say your safe word, then say it." His eyelids narrowed, and he gazed into my eyes.

I was shocked at how strong he'd come on. Reed had been the one who had instructed me, not Kane. Reed was the one I'd been expecting, not Kane.

Kane grabbed my arm. "Come with me, Lea. Now." He marched me down a hallway before I could protest.

The club was emptier than it had been last night, but the few active scenes we passed made me warm.

We came to a metal door with the number eight on it. Kane pulled out some keys from his pocket and unlocked the door. "Go in, little sub."

I took several steps into the room. It was quite large. There was a table loaded with lots of sexual tools. There were a variety of benches, chairs, and chains around the room. There were even bleachers to one side, though there weren't any other people in the room besides Kane and me.

"Close your eyes, trainee."

I felt skittish and shook my head.

"I wasn't giving you a choice. Close. Your. Eyes."

Instantly, I obeyed. The harsher and more demanding his tone, the easier it was for me to comply.

"Good. Keep them closed."

I nodded. Then I felt him stripping me of all my clothes. The air in the room was on the cool side, and I began to tremble.

"Lea, you've got the most amazing ass I've ever seen." I felt his large hands cup my bottom." It's perfect." Kane's tone was deep in his chest and seemed filled with awe.

I wasn't about to fall victim to a smooth-talking player. "I bet you say that to all the women you teach this stuff to."

"You just earned yourself five slaps, trainee." He lifted my arms, and I felt my wrists being encircled with something cold.

I bit my lip, realizing I'd made some kind of mistake. I bowed my head as I'd been taught. "Sir, what did I do wrong?"

He reached around me and pinched my nipples, making them throb and my body hot. He bit my earlobe, and then said in a dangerous pitch that made me shiver, "Two things. One, you didn't address me as 'Sir,' and you didn't trust my words about your hot ass. Do either again and I will add more slaps to your punishment. Understand?"

I gulped. His twin had been gentler with me, though still firm. Kane wasn't keen on fooling around. He meant serious business, and that got me shivering. "Yes, Sir."

"Better, trainee. Much better. Open your eyes," he commanded.

I did.

He guided me to some chains dangling from the ceiling. With such amazing skill, he attached clamps to the chain's rings and then lifted my arms up over my head. I watched him attach the cuffs already on my wrists to the clamps. He stepped back and studied his work. Nodding, apparently pleased by what he saw, Kane knelt down in front of me and attached a bar to each of my ankles. It required that I spread my legs about a foot and a half apart. As anxious excitement took hold of me, I felt my pussy begin to moisten.

Again, Kane circled me several times, gazing at every inch of my body. I knew my curves all too well and wondered why he looked so...pleased by what he saw. Under his stares, I actually almost let myself think I was beautiful. But this was only a lesson. He had a way of teaching that likely drew in the newbie submissive. His gazes were just another part of his training method. That thought got me to wrap a thick, protective wall around my heart. I didn't want to forget that I was only his trainee, his student. Nothing more.

Kane continued his inspection, which was maddening. He wasn't in any kind of hurry to get on with my lesson, and as each second ticked by, my shivers became increasingly intense. Now, even my teeth were chattering, though I wasn't cold. In fact, I was hot, so very hot.

"Perfect," he stated flatly. "Now, what shall I use first?"

I thought about asking for his open hand but instead pressed my lips firmly together.

"What did my brother use on you, trainee?"

"His hand, Sir." I hoped he would, too.

"What else?" he demanded.

"A paddle, Sir." My ass still throbbed a little from last night's spanking from Reed.

"Good to know. I think I'm going to use a cane on your ass, trainee." He stepped to the table directly in front of me. It held a variety of toys.

My heart thudded in my chest, and I blurted out, "I'm not surprised, Sir. It has your same name." Realizing that I'd broken protocol again, I lowered my eyes but got the giggles. It was so inappropriate, like being at a wedding and something gets you snickering where you can't stop.

I caught a glimpse of his smile, which faded fast. He fixed his stare on me, making me jittery. "Don't turn bratty on me, trainee. You've done so well up till now."

I bit my lip and was able to back down the chuckle.

"Now, where was I?" Kane rubbed his chin. "Oh, yes. I'm going to use a cane on you."

I'd read about the use of canes in BDSM play in the literature that Reed had sent home with me. My safe word vibrated on my lips.

As if reading my mind, the gorgeous Dom told me what to expect from the cane.

"Trainee, this is my preferred tool." He picked up the cane on the table and held it up to my eyes. "It has a wicked kiss that you're going to love, but it can also soothe you with a sweet caress."

His knowledge and enthusiasm of the topic was evident to me, and the more he talked, the more wet I became.

"Now, I'm going to use the cane on you to warm up the skin on your ass and thighs. Notice how thin the diameter is on this cane?"

I nodded, afraid if I spoke aloud, my voice would crack.

"This is one of the thinnest canes available. There is a risk to it breaking, but it won't in my hands. I'm very skilled at using any size cane on subs I train."

I wondered how many subs he'd schooled. Thinking there had been likely a hundred or more, my gut tightened from a sudden pang of jealousy. I knew that was foolish, but true all the same. The green-eyed monster inside me grew Hulk-like as I imagined him having a woman in his life already who was not only his trainee but was an actual partner to him. He was too gorgeous of a man not to have someone in his bed at night.

Pushing down my resentment, I concentrated on his enlightenment about caning.

"As Reed told you before, these lessons are about the Dom and submissive relationship and protocols in that dynamic. Remember?"

"Yes, Sir."

"Pain is a tool for both the Dom and sub. It breaks barriers and provides a path to deep trust and understanding. In my hands, the cane isn't just about delivering stings but is more of a sensual toy than a punishment tool." As he continued talking, he touched me softly with the little cane. My skin burned and my nipples throbbed.

Kane flicked my left nipple with the tip of the cane, causing my breast's tips to ache even more. "Regretfully, trainee, many people enter into BDSM and immediately take up things like a cane, which should only be used by a skilled Dom. Without proper education, a cane can cause injury. Not here. Not at The Cell. All Doms must go through rigorous training and education before being allowed to use such a sexual tool. This one is made of bamboo. It delivers its own set of sensations. Now, Reed told you about subspace, correct?"

"Yes, Sir." Normally such a speech would've had me yawning, but not when Kane said it. He sounded so confident and professorial that I knew I could listen to him all night.

Kane swung the cane in the air right in front of me. The thing looked wicked in his hands, and I felt a shiver run up and down my spine. "An untrained Dom might not know that you must keep bamboo canes soaked in salt water to keep them moist. If that isn't done, the cane will splinter and split. Rattan canes are better choices for newbie Doms because they require little care and keep their shape easily."

Continuing to swing the stick in front of me, he went on and on, describing more about caning and how it fit into the BDSM lifestyle. He hadn't even touched me, and I was shaking from head to toe in anxious anticipation of feeling the bamboo on my ass and thighs.

Finally, he ended his delivery of words and cupped my chin. "Are you ready to feel my cane, trainee?"

I choked out, "Yes, Sir."

He gave me a wicked wink and walked behind me.

Without warning, Kane began quickly striking my ass with the bamboo. The hits weren't anything like the paddle had been with Reed, nor were they like his open hand. The cane's stings felt like tiny bites on my bottom.

Tears welled up in my eyes as the tiny stings bit into my skin. It was like he was sending his powerful male energy to me through the cane, demanding surrender. My entire body began to radiate, and my thoughts softened, approaching that wonderful trance-like state I'd felt with Reed last night.

"Very good. You're doing great, trainee." Kane gently rolled the cane up my ass. "This is its embrace. Do you like?"

I nodded as tears streaked down my cheeks.

"It's going to feel differently on your thighs, subbie. It's a nice little bite."

He stung my thighs with quick taps from the bamboo, and he was right. It did feel differently, a bit hotter, making my nerve endings pop to life.

Tap. Tap. Tap. Tap. Tap.

He hit my ass and thighs with rapid-fire, sweet slaps, sending me fully into the subspace he'd mentioned earlier. My face was soaked from tears and my pussy from my juices.

Suddenly, Kane stopped his tempting torture and tugged on my hair. "God, you are such a natural, Lea."

He brought the cane up to my face with his left hand while keeping hold of my locks with his right. In that moment, I felt my surrender. It reminded me of something akin to a long awaited sigh of relief, though I was actually breathing heavily and trembling frantically. It was sweet and joyous. With the bamboo shaft within sight and him tugging on my hair, I trusted Kane with everything. Even in this hypnotic mind frame, I knew it was more than that for me. He'd captured all of me, even my heart.

He let go of my hair and came around in view. He was all smiles, and that pleased me beyond measure. "Subbie, you're learning so very fast."

"Thank you, Sir."

Kane set the cane down on the table. He walked in front of me and cupped my naked breasts. His rugged hands touching my chest thrilled me. "I love your tits, Lea. They are perfect." He began gently massaging my breasts in slow circles with his fingers, making me tingle inside.

Suddenly, he stopped, a frown appearing on his face. "Lesson's over. Let me get you unchained."

My heart sank. "Sir, have I done something wrong?"

He shook his head in the negative, but didn't speak, releasing me from the chains and removing the bar between my legs.

I was frightened by his sudden change, but drifting in and out of the subspace brought on by the cane, I found courage to press him. "Please tell me what is wrong, Sir. I don't want this to end."

One eyebrow shot up, and his eyelids narrowed. "Are you sure about that, trainee? If we continue, I will take this to another level entirely, a more intimate level." His face looked lusty and formidable.

My temperature rose several degrees. "Yes, Sir. I am sure."

The corners of his lips curled up into a smile, swamping my willpower and setting my own want ablaze.

"Let me make myself clear, Lea. You came in here for training, correct?"

"Yes, Sir."

"Now, you want more, right?"

I felt like he was asking these questions in a certain order and in a soft tone for a specific reason. To me, it seemed as if he was guiding me down a path of his choosing. I was more than willing to follow him.

I nodded. "Yes, I want more."

"Then understand this, little sub. Once the lid is off Pandora's box, there is no going back. Not for me. Not for you. I am hot for you, Lea, blistering hot. If you surrender to this, I will devour your body in ways you can't even conceive of yet. Your pussy becomes *my pussy*. Your tits, *my tits*. I'll turn you into a slut who will beg me for more. Most people think my ways are too kinky, too nasty, too demanding, or too strange. For me, it's like breathing. You sure you're ready for that?"

The gravity of what I was committing to hit me in the center of my chest. At risk was my very heart, and yet I'd never wanted anyone more than I wanted Kane right then.

"Yes, Sir." My breaths were shortening to pants. "I-I'm ready."

"Good," he stated flatly, kneeling down right in front of me. I felt his fingers on my pussy, sliding through my wet folds. "Excellent. You shaved. By the feel of your cunt, I'd guess you did it just before coming to the club tonight, right?"

I nodded, shivering and looking at the top of his head below me.

He continued his assault of his digits on my mound, making my body even hotter and my throat even tighter.

"I can't wait to cover your gorgeous pussy with my mouth. I am going to lap up your liquid sweetness, Lea, every single drop. Do you normally shave your cunt?"

His filthy talk ignited cravings inside me, making me even wetter. "No, Sir." Though I did keep myself trimmed up, I'd actually taken a razor to my pussy this morning, as he'd guessed. It had seemed the right thing to do, given I was coming in for my second lesson.

Kane stood up.

Our eyes locked together, and I saw a mix of lust and danger in his. Kane never looked away as he removed his boots, jeans, and the rest of his clothing. I'd seen him without a shirt, but now, with his body fully exposed in front of me, I was astonished at the powerhouse I saw before me. His skin was bronze and glistening from a thin layer of lusty sweat. Kane was cut with muscles that if he'd been a model, could've easily landed him the cover of any workout men's magazine. He was ripped from head to toe. Sporting an eight-pack stomach, he looked like he could take on a dozen men should the need ever arise. Then my eyes caught a glimpse of his cock. The thing was huge. It was clear from his erection, which was massive to say the least, he wanted me.

He pulled me in close and whispered, "I'm going to love watching you squirm, subbie."

My head swam with so many thoughts and my body shivered with even more sensations.

He bit my earlobe as he guided his hands all over my body. He was making his claim on me with every nip and touch. Relenting to him came so natural for me, and I savored every caress, pinch, and bite.

Kane licked my neck and massaged my breasts, and dizziness took hold of my entire being. I couldn't stop shaking. My clit throbbed to the edge of being painful and my pussy moistened till my cream dripped down my inner thighs. God, I was falling for him, which was illogical. This was only training, advanced though it might be, but nothing more. I tried to hold onto that thought with all my might.

"Where are you, subbie?" Kane asked and pinched my nipples harder than any time before, melting all my will.

A tiny cry escaped my mouth. "I-I'm here, Sir."

He released my tips and cupped my chin. "You are now, but you were a million miles away a moment ago. I will not have that, Lea. Ever. You understand that?"

I nodded.

He ran his fingers through my hair, electrifying every cell inside me. Every stroke of his hands in my locks sent me deeper into ecstasy. It might only be fantasy or part of an act, but I couldn't help but lose myself to the dream of being adored by such a delicious man.

"I want to feel those luscious lips around my cock, first." He moved his large hands on my shoulders. "Kneel down, little subbie."

I obeyed.

He tugged on the back of my hair, making me look up into his eyes. "I don't want you to hold back, sub. Show me your best."

I wanted to make him proud and smiled. The bulbous head of his cock was less than an inch from my lips. I extended my tongue and tasted his slick pre-cum. Salty and so very hot, it nearly seared my mouth. Licking the tip in small circles, I hoped to give back to him a little of what he'd already done for me.

"Enough," he growled, and shoved his cock into my mouth.

I breathed through my nose, relaxing my throat the best I could. It worked. I felt his cock slide in even deeper into my mouth. I began sucking hard, hollowing out my cheeks. He thrust his dick into my greedy throat. I tightened my lips on his shaft, which was slipping in and out of my mouth like a piston.

"Fuck, sub. You're sweet lips feel so good on my dick." His hands pressed on the back of my head. "Make me come, subbie. I want to shoot my load down your pretty little throat."

Like a green flag at a race, his words worked to push me on with even more fervor. I sucked and sucked and sucked, readying to drink all he had for me.

"God, yes! Fuck. That's my baby." Kane pulled my head in tighter and the head of his dick crashed hard into the back of my throat. I stopped breathing for a moment, enjoying the feel of his cock in my mouth. The intensity of his dominance over me was overwhelming.

As he shot his load down my throat, my need to have him inside me overwhelmed me. I craved to be stretched, opened, and split in two by him.

After I swallowed the last drop of his seed, he tugged on my hair, pulling me off his dick. As the suction of my mouth released his cock, there was an audible pop.

His hand cradled my chin, and he urged me back on my feet. Kane leaned in and kissed me, making my toes curl and my insides tingle.

As he ended our kiss, his fingers feathered up and down my sides. As his stare fixed on me, I felt a shiver shoot up my back. "My sweet cocksucker. Time for me to taste your sweet desserts."

He led me back to one of the chairs in the room. I sat down, and he cuffed my wrists and ankles to the D-clamps attached to the chair.

Being restrained by him was becoming more and more natural to me. In fact, I enjoyed the feeling it brought out in me. Being with Kane was so easy, so real, and so very, very hot.

When his head dipped between my legs, I began breathing in half breaths.

"I've never seen a more perfect cunt in my life, sub. I love my cunt." He exhaled a hot blast of air over my swollen folds, and my half breaths became tiny gasps and pants.

He kissed my thighs, sending a delicious rush that flattened me. I was crazed for more. I thrashed in the chair as his tongue danced up my leg and near my clit, almost... almost... almost... but never quite touching. The distress was driving me mad, and still his torture went on and on.

Kane grabbed my knees and forced them farther apart from each other. His kisses turned to wicked bites that raised my temperature to a blistering level. I thought I would go completely insane if he didn't take me soon. When his fingers threaded through my swollen, soaked folds, I was trembling like a live wire.

"That's my baby." He growled. "I love seeing you suffer."

He licked me into a frenzied passionate haze and sent his fingers into my pussy. My insides clenched and unclenched around his digits. My want swamped me. At that very moment, nothing would suffice or quell my need but his cock seated inside my body.

Kane twisted his fingers inside my pussy, stretching me for his thick dick. He clasped my clit between his teeth, delivering a sweet sting that sent me reeling. I bit my lip at the hurt, but still shifted my hips up into his hungry mouth.

"That's my little subbie. You like this?"

"Y-yes, Sir," I confessed.

"This is fucking nothing. This is playing with you. This is getting the sweet slut inside you warmed up." He looked up at me with his dangerous, dark eyes, and a tremor shot through me. "Lea, you're going to come and come, but it won't be enough. I'm going to fill you up again and again. You'll plead and beg, but I won't stop until you are completely thrashed."

His words were like hot, passionate bombs that detonated my very core. The world had vanished with each lusty syllable from his thick lips, and all that remained was my overwhelming need for him.

"Please, Sir," I begged. "Please."

He pressed his thumb on my clit, making me moan. It was too much, too powerful. I couldn't stand any more. "Tell me, subbie. What do you want?"

I screamed, unable to hold back any longer. "You! I want you, Sir!"

He pinched my inner thighs, making me yelp. "Tell me."

"I want your dick inside me...inside my pussy."

"That's my baby." Kane moved a lever, and the chair reclined back far, becoming more of a bench with arms.

He stood and walked to the table where he grabbed a condom package. I watched him roll the rubber down his long, thick cock and felt my heart race.

"You know what this is?" he asked, holding an odd-looking toy.

I shook my head.

"This is a plug for your tight ass. Have you ever had your ass fucked, subbie?"

"No, Sir," I answered, anxiety welling up like the rising tide.

"Good to know." He applied some lube to the plug. With a lusty smile pasted across his face, he walked back to me. "Time for more agony, sub. Understand? Lay back."

I nodded and did as he asked, tears brimming my eyelids, brought on not from worry but from surrender to Kane.

He slathered some lube on his fingers and shoved his hand under my ass. His hands shot between my legs and under me. I felt him finger my tight entrance, and I thought I might pass out. I didn't, of course, but my worry didn't subside. As he pierced through into my ass, I swallowed a deep breath and held it in my lungs. The initial pain his fingers had brought went down quickly. Over and over, he stretched my ass, making it ready for the plug. I wasn't sure such a large thing could get past my tightness, but I trusted Kane to know.

"You're ready for the plug, subbie. Breathe in and out slowly. Don't hold your breath," he instructed. "Understand?"

"Yes, Sir. In and out. Slowly. Got it, Sir."

He smiled, and I took in my first lungful of air, and then another.

As I let the last cubic inch of breath past my lips, Kane shoved the toy into my ass, delivering instant and powerful pain.

"Ride it out, baby. You can do it."

As tears streaked down my cheeks, I chewed on my lip. Soon the hurt was gone and so was the last bit of my resistance. I could feel the toy in my ass, stretching me beyond what I thought was even possible. I entered a trance-like state, and my thoughts quieted to a whisper. My body, on the other hand, screamed and burned.

"It's in, subbie." He kissed my cheeks gently, and I melted under him. "You're doing great, Lea."

Kane unfastened my cuffs from the chair's D-clamps. He crawled on top of me, and I could feel his erection press on my mound. Shifting his body, he positioned the head of his cock on my opening. I gasped when he thrust his nine inches into my pussy. I was so close, my climax bubbling beneath the surface.

"Wrap your legs around my waist, Lea."

I obeyed instantly.

He continued, "Now, hold on to the arms of this chair and squeeze them tight."

Mere seconds from release, I clutched the chair tightly, praying he would topple me over the edge and into orgasm.

He shoved his cock in deeper into my pussy, and my trembles intensified. "Nice, tight cunt. Clench my dick, sub. Make me feel you."

Again, I complied. I could feel his cock massaging my insides, hitting the perfect spot in my channel. I writhed under him, and I shot my arms up to his shoulders, scraping his flesh with my nails.

"Come for me, Lea. Come now."

His words released the orgasmic avalanche inside me. Spasms in my womb shook my whole body. I screamed.

Kane shoved his cock in and out of my pussy. His eyes seemed to glaze over as his final and deepest thrust took hold of him. "Fuuuck!" he yelled as he came inside me.

The full weight of his body came down on me, pinning me even tighter to the chair. I shivered frantically, giving in to the sensations still firing in my own body.

Kane kissed me. It felt so right to be in his arms. There wasn't another place in the entire world I would rather have been.

After a bit, he stood up. He removed the plug from my ass. "You did great, trainee. Really great."

Something in his tone worried me. He sounded distant.

"Thank you, Sir," I answered, feeling the walls reassemble around my heart. Foolishly, I'd led with my feelings in this training. There was no one to blame but me for the inevitable heartache to come.

Feb 12th

I'm still in the bed, and it's two in the afternoon.

I've gotten texts and voicemails from both Kane and Reed.

I am so fucked.

My eyes are swollen from crying over two men I only met the night before last. My finance of four years didn't even get a single tear out of me when he told me it was over. Now, I'm a complete basket case.

I wish I could sort this out, but I just can't. I wish I knew what was wrong with me. My head is so mixed up.

I'm already having feelings for both of them, God help me.

They may look alike but they are so different. Sure, they are both Dominants, but Reed has a tender side that Kane doesn't. And yet, I am drawn to both of them equally. See, I am fucked. Fucked up, anyway.

Last night with Kane was amazing. But so was the night before with Reed.

Shit. My cell phone again. Why won't they give up? I am not going back to that club ever.

It was Kane again. His texts are getting more and more demanding. This one was, *Call me now, Lea. Right now.* I can imagine how angry he must be getting, but I just can't face him or Reed. Choosing one or the other isn't something I want to deal with. My best plan of action is to stay away from them before I fall even deeper. If I don't, I risk having my heart ripped completely apart.

For them, I'm sure I'm just another new sub to train. For me, they are much more than they should be.

Even if there is a million-to-one shot for me with one of them for something more, how could I ever choose between Kane and Reed? I couldn't.

Not now. Not ever.

ABOUT EIGHT-THIRTY, Reed was banging on my door, demanding I let him in. Afraid my neighbors might call the police, I cracked open the door.

"Reed, I'm in no condition to see you right now."

His eyelids narrowed. "Are you sick?"

"Not exactly." My heart was racing in my chest. I didn't want to face him. It was too much.

"Let me in, Lea. We need to talk."

"I just can't."

"You can." His tone softened, and his eyes widened. "Five minutes, pet. If after that you want me to leave, I will."

Unlatching the chain, I was shocked at how quickly I slipped into wanting to obey him. More than that, I wanted one more time to be alone with him—even if it was for only five minutes. Before I opened the door wide, I looked down at my robe and realized what an awful state I was in. "Wait, Reed. I'm not even dressed."

He shoved the door open and cupped my chin. "I've seen you in less, Lea."

"I-I know, but not without m-makeup," I stammered.

"You look amazing to my eyes, sweetheart." He never let go of my face, and his touch was making my temperature rise.

"You're lying, of course, but thank you."

"You're very welcome, my love."

"Please, Reed. Stop." My head was spinning with confusion. Just being so near him threatened to overwhelm me. I needed him to go and fast. "You wanted five minutes. The clock is ticking."

He pulled his hand back, releasing my chin. "What the fuck did Kane do to you, Lea?"

I closed my eyes tight, fighting back the tears that threatened to fall. "Nothing. Your brother did nothing wrong."

"Don't lie to me, Lea. Our time together was great. You were great." His voice shook with apparent rage. "One lesson with him and you won't take my calls or answer my texts. Something happened, and I want to know what it was."

I opened my eyes and felt the tears streak down my face. "You want to know? Fine. I'll tell you. Kane opened me up even more. He was amazing. That's the problem, Reed. Can't you see?"

Without another word, Reed leaned in and kissed me silent. I sobbed into his embrace, feeling his tongue sweep into my mouth. He lifted me up into his arms, never releasing my lips. I wrapped my arms around his thick neck, my resistance vanishing. Why was my willpower absent whenever he was next to me?

As if he already knew my apartment, he carried me into my bedroom.

Somehow I found my voice. "We shouldn't do this, Reed."

He lowered my back down to my mattress. "We should and we must, sweetheart. I can see now that Kane took things further than normal in your lesson with him." He removed my robe, and I shivered, not from the cold but from being wonderfully exposed in front of him. "Time to put things right and let you know how I feel about you."

"I don't understand, Reed."

"I'm much better at showing than telling, Lea. You're about to find out a whole bunch about me."

I covered my face with both hands. "This is foolish. I can't do this."

He grabbed my wrists, gently tugging my arms down to my sides. "Time for another lesson, sub."

"A lesson? Now?"

"Yes. Now. Look me in the eyes," he commanded.

I obeyed, gazing into his light brown eyes and feeling my need to

LEE SWIFT & KRIS COOK

surrender just under the surface. I realized how much alike he and Kane looked. "Reed, I'm confused. Maybe we should—"

"Let go, Lea. Remember the protocols I taught you?"

I nodded.

"This is a scene. Time to follow the protocols. Understand?"

My jaw dropped. "Here? Reed, you have to be joking."

He frowned and pinched both my nipples, delivering a sting that told me he wasn't kidding around. "Right here. Right now. Our scene. Alone. Understand, sub?"

The strangest thing happened inside me that very moment. It was like my most natural instinct clicked in—an instinct to obey. More than that, I was already pulling up the fantasy of Reed and Kane paddling my ass simultaneously. Right or wrong, I wanted to please Reed and have one last night with him. "Yes, Sir."

"This lesson is about you letting go and latching on to pleasure." Reed's big hands slid up and down my sides, causing a spark to zip through my body. I trembled, feeling my skin tingle.

Though filled with both confusion and excitement, I somehow found the tiniest speck of hesitation still inside me to latch on to. "We should talk about this first, don't you think?"

"I told you that I'm better showing than telling." His voice vibrated deep in his chest, shaking me to my core. "What state are you in?"

"Good...I mean green, or maybe yellow. No, I believe I'm green, Sir. But seriously, I think this is the wrong thing to do."

"Either you're green or you're not." His fingertips skimmed my body like feathers, lighting up my skin like fireworks on a Fourth of July night. "Which is it?"

I sighed, giving in to my surrender to him. "Green, Sir. I'm definitely green."

"Follow our protocols, little sub." His self-confidence spoke to me on so many levels. He wasn't asking to come to my bed; he was demanding it. "Don't get sidetracked. Understand?"

"Yes, Sir," I said, vowing that this would have to be the last time with him. One night of utter ecstasy was all I could hope for. After tonight, no more. Since I was going to sample his wicked pleasures once more, I asked, "Are you going to do what you did to me on my first lesson?"

"Yes and no."

"I'm not sure I understand," I admitted.

"I'm going to spank you for not answering my calls or returning my texts. Unlike the lesson, your spanking will be for punishment."

"I'm sorry, Sir. I really am."

He kissed me tenderly. "I know you are, but you're still unsure about what to do with me, with Kane, with all of it. I'm going to help you through that. But first, you need to take your thirty slaps to that pretty ass. Roll over, Lea."

I gulped. "Thirty? My ass is still sore from my two lessons at The Cell. Please, Sir. I-I am really sorry."

"Keep giving me lip, sub, and I'll make it forty. Understand?"

"Okay. Yes, Sir." I rolled over on my stomach and braced myself for the punishment to come.

Reed took the tie of my robe and wrapped my wrists together with it. Then he took the remaining part of the tie and fastened it to one of my bedposts. "This will keep you secure. You have another robe in your closet, Pet?"

Trembling, I nodded.

He went to my closet and came back with my pale blue silk robe. Using its tie to restrain my legs, he wrapped it around my ankles and hooked it up to another bedpost. "Perfect."

I could bend my knees and elbows slightly but didn't have any real range of motion left to me save to writhe and thrash.

Reed's hand came down on my ass with a crack, and a hot sting spread over my flesh. With the pain came an equal dose of desire, too.

He leaned down and whispered in my ear, "When I call, sub, you will answer. When I text, you will text me back."

Slap. Whimpering, I felt myself stiffen. How could I take his calls or texts? This had to be the end. There was no other alternative.

Slap. Slap. Slap. I tugged on my ties, chewing on my lower lip.

The more his hand rained down on my ass, the closer I came to that sweet subspace he and Kane had introduced me to. As the heat seared my backside, I began to sob, slipping into a trance, releasing all my worries and fears, if only for this moment. I floated in the expanse, relishing the sensations firing in my body. The stings were morphing into pleasure fast, and I loved every second of it. I'd been counting his spanks, but lost track sometime after his tenth smack to my ass.

"That's my girl. Ride this out, baby." His hand hit my ass again and again, and I melted into each and every one of them.

"That was thirty, sub." He cupped my ass with one hand and fingered my pussy with the other. Heat flamed through me. "You're soaked, pet."

I felt hot blood fill my cheeks.

"I'm going to enjoy lapping up your sweet cream, baby." He unfastened the ties from my bedposts. "Roll over on your back."

Unable to refuse him, I obeyed.

Then he refastened the ties back to the posts, restraining me once again. "That'll hold you, pet." Reed leaned over and kissed me on the neck, sending several shivers through my body.

His next kiss landed on my mouth, sending its message of possession to me loud and clear. I clenched and unclenched my fists, mirroring what was happing deep inside me.

He moved down my body until his thick lips feathered my chest, causing me to get even wetter. When he swallowed one of my nipples and pinched the other one, I panted. I was a livewire of feminine sensations. He licked and sucked on my tips until they were throbbing and elongated. I was unable to hold back my passionate moans.

Reed kissed my stomach softly, causing gooseflesh to pop up there. When his tongue circled my navel, I actually thought I might go insane.

When I felt his lips on my clit, I held my breath. Sure, he'd spanked me the other night, but having his face right next to my sex was overwhelming me to the max.

"God, this is the prettiest cunt I've ever seen." I felt his hands on my thighs and began whimpering uncontrollably.

I needed him to touch me, to take away some of my suffering. If he didn't soon, I wasn't sure how I would survive. "Please, Sir. I can't take much more."

"You've earned your reward, pet." She heard him inhale deeply.

"God, Lea, I love your scent. You smell like strawberries and morning mist."

Even the way he talked about me was increasing my cravings. I needed relief in the worst way, but all I could do tied to the bedposts was fist my sheets and scream. When his tongue slid through my weeping sex, I did both.

"Such sweet pussy cream," he muttered, licking me into oblivion.

His oral lesson went on and on for some time, until I was certain I would pass out soon from the sheer volume of my need. His hands slid up my thighs, spreading me wider. His tongue shot down into my channel, and one of his fingers pressed with the perfect pressure on my clit. My entire body stiffened, and my half breaths came fast and furious. I was nearing release.

Reed stood and stripped off his clothes. I gasped when I looked at his thick, erect cock. Unable to take my eyes from him, I watched him don a condom on his shaft.

He looked like a predator about to pounce. "Time to fill your tight, pretty cunt with my dick, sweetheart."

He crawled on top of me and thrust his cock into my pussy, stretching my insides to the limit. The friction of his shaft against my G-spot got me even closer to falling over the edge.

His thrusts were deep and slow, enhancing my trembles. In and out. Over and over. Again and again. So many sensations were stacking up inside me with each of Reed's plunges into my pussy, begging for satisfaction. I was mad for release.

"Come for me, sub." He reached between our bodies, sending his fingertips to my clit. Then he rubbed the sensitive bundle fast and hard, continuing to plunge his dick into my pussy

I screamed as my insides burst into flames, rising higher and higher. Every cell sparked to life in me. As spasms shook me from head to toe, I couldn't stay still no matter how hard I tried. Instinctively, I squeezed my pussy around his dick. My back arched off the mattress, and I screamed again.

"Yes. Yes. Yes." Reed growled low, sounding like a man at the end of his rope about to be swamped by an unstoppable flood.

Then I felt his cock jerk violently inside me. Knowing he was coming, I clenched my pussy as hard as I could around his dick.

"Fuuuck!" he yelled, succumbing to his climax and covering my body with his own.

His weight was holding me in place more than the ties on my wrists and ankles were. Still, I loved the feeling of him on top of me.

I was still trembling from my own orgasm when Reed rolled off of me and removed my restraints. Then he shifted to his side, pulling my back into his front until we were locked together in a tight spoon.

Even in my muddled state, one question shot to the forefront of my consciousness.

What the hell have I done?

I should have avoided Reed at all cost, hunkering down quietly behind my door at his earlier insistent pounding for me to open up for him. Now, I was in so deep I would never make it back to the surface for a breath.

Reed whispered in my ear. "Where are you, Lea? You seem miles away,"

"This is all just... I'm not sure..." I sighed, feeling the heaviness in my heart. "I don't know what to say."

"Try, love."

"Like that." Tears welled up in my eyes as my mind brought up an image of Kane in his full-on Dom attire.

"Like what?"

"When you call me 'love' or 'pet' it confuses me."

"I don't understand."

"Of course you don't. How could you? It's me. I'm the one who is fucked up." I tried to get free of his hold but couldn't as he tightened his grip on me.

"Lea, you're not fucked up. You're incredible. I've never been with anyone like you. You're brave, smart, sexy, and so much more."

I sobbed. "Please. Don't say anything else. I can't take it."

"I came here to say something to you, and by damn I'm going to say it. Face me," he ordered.

I twisted around to him. We were so close that I could feel his breath on my face. His eyes were unblinking from the clear gravity of what he was about to tell me.

"Now listen to me. It's crazy, I know. We've only known each other for a couple of days, but that doesn't change the fact that in that short time, you've been all I can think about. I'm sorry about missing your second lesson. I fucked up."

"Kane told me about your dog. You had to deal with that."

"Maybe so, but I should have called you and cancelled the lesson. Instead, I asked Kane to take over. Tell me the truth, Lea. Did he fuck you?"

I closed my eyes, fearing the worst.

"Answer me, pet. Please."

"Yes, Reed. Your brother and I had sex."

"Kane's an asshole. Damn it."

I opened my eyes and kissed Reed, hoping to soften his rage. "He's not an asshole, and neither are you. You want the truth? Here it is. I've fallen for both of you. Maybe it's only a rebound from my ex, or maybe it's something more. But I can't continue down this path any longer. I just can't."

"Shh, Lea. Listen to me."

I had to make him understand. "No. This isn't a scene. This is real life. Please, Reed. You've shown me so much. I will be forever grateful to you and Kane for that."

"Lea, I think I'm falling for you." Reed's admission melted my insides.

My own new feelings for him could easily latch onto his words, but I knew that would only end in disaster. Even if Kane didn't feel the same for me as Reed, I definitely felt the same for him as I did his twin.

"That means a lot to me, Reed, but it can't be. No doubt about it, I already care for you, too. You *think* you are falling in love with me, and maybe if we could continue with whatever this is, our feelings for each other might actually turn into something real."

"Exactly." Under his confident surface, I saw a panic that mirrored my own. "Give *us* a chance, Lea."

I shook my head. "I can't. This isn't just about you and me."

"Do you mean Kane?" His face darkened.

"Yes. I have feelings for him, too. So, you see, this can never be."

"Why not? Spend more time with me and you'll see I'm the one for you, not him. Hell, spend more time with Kane and you'll see he's not someone who you'd ever want to build a life with."

"Stop it, Reed. This is hard enough for me." Tears streamed down my cheeks. "Even if I could find it in my heart to choose one of you, can you imagine what that would do to you and Kane? It would rip you two apart. Don't even try to deny it. I tell you I care about him and you start telling me why it would never work. I'm not going to do this any longer."

"Lea, you're not responsible for how Kane and I deal with each other."

I left the bed and put on my robe. "I can't choose between you and Kane. It's just not possible. Please, Reed. I'm dying inside right now."

"Let's talk this out, baby."

"You told me you weren't much of a talker. Right now, neither am I. You need to go. Your five minutes is up."

"Okay, Lea. But I need to apply some cream to your ass."

"No," I said harshly. Softening my tone, I continued, "I can take care of that myself."

"Sure, sweetheart. I'll go now. But I'm not giving up on *us*. You'll see. Believe me."

I wanted to believe him more than anything, but I knew things for me would end badly no matter how much I wished for something different.

As he dressed, I vowed to myself that no matter how hard the brothers tried to get me to see them, I would refuse. There would be no more nights at The Cell and no more nights with the two men who had captured all of me. My heart might not survive my new vow, but I wasn't about to come between Reed and Kane. Ever.

Feb 13th

Ever since Reed left last night, I've been an utter mess. I haven't been able to sleep or eat or anything.

Did I make a mistake pushing him away? No. It was the right thing to do, but it fucking hurts so much.

~

My cell phone exploded this morning.

Six more texts and two voicemails from Kane are waiting for me to read and listen to. I can't face his words. Reed has called three times but hasn't left any messages.

Daniel, my only brother and the eldest of my siblings and me, is great for any legal and financial questions, but for things of the heart, I know the experts are my sisters, Ella and Amy. Needing female confidants to talk this out with, I've called both of them. I'd thought about calling Mia, but wondered if she might be too close to the situation to be able to really listen. And though Misty, Mia's sister, and I are really close, of all of us, she's the most uptight. I am in no condition to hear recriminations from her.

Hell, I know I screwed everything up.

I'm not actually looking for answers. I just need some friendly shoulders to cry on.

~

ELLA AND AMY sat on either side of me, wrapping their arms around my body as I sobbed and sobbed. I was still in my robe, my hair looking Medusa-ish. I was quite a contrast to my sisters.

Ella wore a navy blue business suit and designer heels. Her blonde hair looked amazing in the new bob cut that reminded me of Victoria Beckham's. Amy's hair was blonde with bright pink highlights. Her flowing pale yellow dress and matching sandals mirrored her always sunny attitude. Sure they were on opposite sides of the fashion wheel, but they both were stunning in their own right.

It took a while for me to tell them the whole story about Reed and Kane, but they didn't push me, letting me take all the time I needed. When I was done, I felt like I'd run an emotional marathon. I was completely wrung out.

"Sweetie, this is likely a rebound." Ella squeezed my hand. "Jerry just broke up with you."

If only that were true. "I thought it might be, sis, but it feels so much deeper than anything I ever had with Jerry. I did love him, but it wasn't anything like this. It was safe and comfortable."

"Sounds like the phone call you and I had last summer about your sex life with Jerry—safe and comfortable." Amy never held back. She was an open book and never understood why everyone else wasn't. "Right, Lea?"

"Yes. Boring."

"No wonder you're smitten with Reed and Kane." Amy smiled. "They sound exciting and dangerous. Bad boys are every girl's fantasy."

"I'm not just smitten. I know it sounds crazy, but I've already fallen head over heels for them."

Ella sighed. "Scratch my rebound theory. Sweetie, are you sure you aren't more into one or the other? It would make things much simpler for you."

"I like where you're going with this, Ella." Amy brightened. "Team Reed or Team Kane. Which is it, Lea?"

"Both. Don't you get it? I care about both of them. I could never choose. Ever."

A knock on the door startled all of us.

Amy jumped up before I could stop her. "I hope it's one of your guys, Lea. Or maybe both of them."

I couldn't face them now. "Don't answer the door."

Just like when we were kids, Amy totally disregarded my directions and opened the door.

Thankfully, the people standing in the doorway weren't Reed or Kane. Instead, Mia and Misty walked in, their faces full of concern.

I smiled weakly. "If I knew we were going to have a party, I would've dressed."

Misty came and sat beside me in the spot that Amy had just vacated. "Honey, I came as soon as Amy called."

I glared at my youngest sister. "You're going to pay."

She shrugged. "I'm sorry, sis, but this is hard. I knew you needed all of us."

"You didn't call Daniel, too?"

Amy grinned broadly. "Love our big brother, but no. This is way out of his league."

Mia stood in front of me. "I feel responsible for all of this, Lea. I'm so sorry."

Mia had been so happy since meeting Lex. I didn't want her to feel bad. "You didn't do this to me, sweetie. I went to your boyfriend's club because I wanted to go. I'm a grown woman. This is all on me, not you."

"How about I put on a pot of tea?" Misty asked.

"Screw that, girlfriend." Amy walked into my kitchen, which was open to the living room. "This calls for adult beverages." She opened a couple of cabinets. "Where's your booze, sis?"

Even though my heart was in tatters, I was happy to have my sisters and cousins with me. It didn't take the pain away, but it did make it more tolerable, at least for the moment. "If I have any, it's in the cabinet next to the sink."

Amy pulled out a couple of bottles of wine, one white and one red. Her arm went to the back of the cabinet. "Come to mama." Her hand came back with a bottle of tequila.

"Are we sure this is what Lea needs right now?" Misty asked in her most motherly tone.

"She's a big girl, cousin. We all are." Amy laughed. "You could use a few shots yourself to loosen you up, Misty, if you ask me."

"I'm not asking you," she barked back. "And I'll have you know I've drank margaritas before. Several times."

"Sounds promising. Shot glasses, Lea?"

"Wall cabinet to the left of the stove."

Amy nodded, pulling out five tiny glasses. "Misty, you game?"

Misty looked directly in my eyes. "If Lea is, I am."

"I'll have a shot." I tried to mask my agony but even I could hear the suffering in my tone. "What can it hurt now?"

With Amy's encouragement, we all did three shots of the liquid gold. I was beginning to feel fuzzy around the edges. The pain was still there in the background, but the tequila helped me keep it back. Still, I knew if I let myself, I could succumb to another round of tears for the loss I felt. My company talked about several ways to get me out of my funk. They even started planning a trip to the Caribbean. I nodded and smiled, drifting back into my quiet despair. Nothing would ever be the same for me, no matter how much each of them said it would. Reed and Kane had changed me forever. I knew no man could ever open me up the way they had. The vibrancy of the life I'd peaked at with Reed and Kane was gone. The only future I could expect now was dull, gray, and so very cold.

Another knock on the door and the chatter around me stopped.

In a hushed tone, I threatened, "Amy, I swear if you open that door I will never forgive you."

From the other side of the door, a voice I recognized was a relief.

"Mia, open the door," Lex stated flatly.

"Ask him if he's alone," Misty requested. I hadn't thought about the possibility that Reed and Kane might be with him, so I was glad that she had.

"Are you by yourself, Lex?" Mia asked.

"Yes."

Mia swung the door open. "Hi, sweetheart."

Lex stood in the doorway looking stunningly sexy in jeans and a black sweater. "Did you tell Lea what I have planned?"

"What plan?" I snapped.

He held up his hand but didn't turn away from Mia.

"No, Sir. I did just what you said and waited for you to come."

He leaned in and kissed her. "That's my, baby."

Ella stood up and extended her hand in her normal corporate flair. "You must be the guy that swept my cousin off her feet."

"Yes, I am. You're Ella, right?" He took her hand and shook it.

I could tell Ella was impressed that he knew her name. "The one and only. I'm happy to meet you."

"That remains to be seen, Ella." Lex looked at my youngest sister next. "You are?"

"Amy. But I bet you already knew that, too, didn't you?" She smiled and took his hand.

"So that means you must be Mia's sister." Lex offered his hand to Misty.

Misty nodded but didn't take it.

The corners of Lex's mouth curled up. "Just like I imagined."

Then he turned to me. "Hello, Lea."

I choked out, "Hi, Lex. This is more of a female party. I'm not sure why you're here."

He sat down on the travel chest that was doubling as my coffee table. He grabbed both my hands. "You're about to find out. In fact, all of you are."

I'm not sure if it was the tequila or the fatigue, but I couldn't argue with him. I wanted to hear him out.

The others must've been in the same frame of mind, as all I could hear was my own breath.

Mia came and sat beside him. He handed my left hand to her to hold while keeping my right hand in his.

Trembling, I said, "Tell me, please."

Lex nodded. "Okay. First, I know Kane screwed up with you."

"No. It's not like that, Lex."

"Quiet, Lea. Hear me out. Kane came to me and told me what happened. I found it odd that he took things too far with you since he and Reed are the best trainers I have at the club. Sex shouldn't have been on the table for your second lesson. Not yet. I'd made it clear to both of them what I expected with you."

"What was that?"

"To test you and see if you and your cousin here had similar tastes." He patted Mia on the leg. "I thought you might be like her the second I met you, Lea. You're a submissive, all right."

"This is crazy talk," Misty snapped. "I can't believe any of this."

Lex turned to her but didn't say a word. Apparently, his stare alone was enough to silence Misty.

After what seemed like minutes, Lex turned his eyes back to me. "Like I was saying, I'd set up your training in a very specific order. Reed followed my instructions for your first lesson, though he told me it was very difficult for him."

"How?" I recalled how amazing it had been to surrender to him and feel his paddle and hand on my ass. "I did what he said that night. Every command."

Lex snorted. "You're definitely a sub. Yes, you did. Reed found it difficult to follow my instructions. He wanted to make love to you the moment you two were alone in the training room, but he was able to keep his head. That would've been the end of it if he hadn't fucked up when he came here last night."

"He told you about our time together?"

"You're still under my care, Lea. I'm responsible for you."

The contract I'd signed was for the club. Why would he think he was responsible for me at home? "At The Cell, sure. I get that. But not here, Lex. Not now."

Lex shook his head. "Yes, here. Yes, now. That hasn't changed. It won't until you select a Dom to take my place."

Misty's jaw dropped. "You mean to fuck her and my sister?"

Lex grabbed her by the arm. "There's a nasty slut inside you, Misty, just waiting to be let out, isn't there?"

"I-I don't know what you're talking about." By her tone, I knew she did, which didn't surprise me much. Misty had shared several of her fantasies with me when we had been teens. They were quite incongruent for the uptight woman she'd become.

"The answer is 'no,' Misty. Her being under my care doesn't have anything to do with sex." Lex's tone was so male, so confident, and so powerful. "Understand?"

Misty nodded and then looked down at her hands. Apparently, he'd hit some nerve inside her.

Lex turned back to me. "No more talking except between me and Lea. Do you all understand me?"

They all squeaked the affirmative.

"Good. Interruptions drive me crazy." He gazed at me for the longest time before speaking. Finally he said, "Do you love them, Lea?"

Tears streamed down my face. "Yes, Lex. I love them. My heart is crushed. They didn't do anything wrong. I did. I wanted to be with them, to feel beautiful and adored. They gave me that and so much more. Please don't blame them. It's all my fault, not theirs."

Lex sighed. "No wonder they fucked up my lessons with you, Lea. You're quite a woman. I think you are right, though. You are to blame some in this. So, here's what you're going to do. Kane deserves to hear what you told Reed last night."

I couldn't go through that again. "I can't tell him good-bye. It was hard enough with Reed. Kane knows, doesn't he?"

Lex's voice was commanding. "You can, Lea. You will, too. Yes, Kane knows, but you have to tell him yourself, in person."

"Please, Lex," I begged. "Don't make me do this."

I saw compassion in Lex's eyes. "Kiddo, I don't want to make you suffer any more than you already have, but you must face this. If you don't, you'll regret this for the rest of your life."

I knew he was right. "Okay. Where? When?"

"Tomorrow night. I'll send a limo. You'll get through this, Lea. I promise."

"If she's going, so am I," Misty blurted. "I'm not letting her face this alone."

Lex laughed. "My club, Misty. My rules. You'll get your chance soon enough."

Feb 14th

I walked beside Lex in one of the hallways of The Cell. I'd refused to dress in any of Viv's outfits, preferring my own clothes—jeans, top, and tennis shoes. I knew I looked more appropriate for the grocery store or doing laundry than for this exclusive club, but I didn't care. What I'd come for wouldn't take long, or at least I hoped it wouldn't.

I was exhausted. Lex was taking me to face something that had kept me awake most of the night. Three nights of little sleep was taking its toll on me, but I knew what I had to do no matter how tired I was.

Lex had been right. Kane deserved to hear from me why I wasn't coming back for his lessons.

Shaking violently, I continued trekking beside Mia's man. I wasn't sure what to say, but I hoped it would come to me when I saw Kane.

"We're here," The Cell's owner announced when we came to the last door on the left of the hallway. It was slightly ajar. I trembled, knowing who was waiting for me inside.

"Thank you, Lex. I'm sorry about all of this. Please don't blame Reed and Kane."

He pulled me in tight and gave me a brotherly hug. "Just get inside,

Lea. Everything is ready for you. And Mia is waiting for me in the Egyptian room." He rubbed his hands together. "Time for me to enjoy a night with my sweetheart."

Lex turned and headed back down the hallway from which we'd come. I opened the door wider and entered the room.

It was spectacular. Unlike the training room where I'd spent time with Reed and Kane, this space was tricked out for the members to enjoy their scene in a fantastic setting. The illusion sent me back to a regal time.

This could've been the bedroom of the daughter of a very powerful and rich king. Marble floors, beautiful tapestries, and dark mahogany furnishings transported me to the Renaissance of Europe. I looked even more out of place here than I had in the hallway.

There was no sign of Kane, so I sat down on the big comfy bed with its massive posts and accompanying canopy. I wondered why Lex had chosen this room for our meeting. Perhaps it was the only one free. The Cell was a very busy place.

Where was Kane? Even as nervous as I was, my fatigue took hold of me, and I yawned.

That first exhale of weary air was followed by several more, one after the other. My eyelids were heavy. I stretched out on the bed...

∽

"LEA," Kane's voice wafted through my dreamy state.

I smiled, recalling how wonderful he'd been to me. Everything about him made me vibrate with desire. He was powerful, impatient, and so wonderful. All I wanted to do was to please him.

"Wake up, Lea," Reed's voice drifted in my head.

I sighed, seeing an image of the sexy man appear in front of me. Tender but firm, demanding but generous, Reed's mix called to me on so many levels.

The dream was wonderful. They both gazed down at me, making me believe in fairy tales. In my dreams, I didn't have to choose. In here, they were mine, both of them, and I was theirs.

I reached up to touch their faces and suddenly realized that I wasn't asleep. This was real.

"What is this?" I gasped.

"Hush, baby." Reed leaned down and kissed me, his long hair tickling my cheeks. "Just listen."

"No. I'm here to tell Kane something. I have to tell him, Reed. He deserves to hear it from me."

Reed smiled and sat up. "She's all yours, bro."

I gazed into Kane's eyes. He wasn't smiling. "Me first, sub. Then, Reed. Then, you. Understand?"

I thought about objecting, but couldn't. If only for a few more minutes, I was willing to surrender to his control.

"Good. I never expected someone like you to come into my life, Lea." Kane stroked the side of my face with his fingertips. "I thought I'd always be a resident Dom, either here or at some other club. Something permanent and exclusive never entered into the realm of what was even possible for me—until you. I've always believed in lust at first sight but not love. That only happens in the movies. Or so I thought. Did you wonder why I volunteered so quickly to teach that class to the new members your first night at The Cell?"

I'd figured he couldn't possibly be interested in someone like me, but I decided not to mention that. "No."

"The minute I met you, Lea, all I could think of was how I was going to get you into my bed, not for one night, or two, but for always. I'd never felt anything like it before. Later, I rationalized that it had been some crazy, fiery lust that had taken ahold of me. Made sense. You're curvy in just the spots I enjoy. But when I came to train you, that feeling hadn't gone away at all. The more I learned about you that night and what made you tick, the more crazed I was to possess you for myself."

I put my hands up to my face, wiping tears from my eyes. "It's hopeless. I care for you, too. But I also care for Reed, and he's told me he feels the same. There's no way through this without someone getting hurt."

Kane grabbed my wrists and gently pulled them down. "Sure there is, sweetheart."

"How? One of you backs down after I make an impossible choice? I won't do it. I won't. I won't." I closed my eyes tight. My lips were trembling from the gravity of what I was confessing, but I wasn't about to mislead them any more.

"Open your eyes," he commanded.

I complied with more tears brimming.

"Look at our little sub, Reed. Isn't she something else?" Kane asked, smiling.

Reed nodded, "She sure is, bro. Enough talk. Let's show her."

"Agreed." Kane squeezed onto the bed next to me.

"Show me what?" I asked.

Kane kissed me into silence, his tongue sweeping inside my mouth like a conquering hero. My heart thudded in my chest, and my toes curled. As he continued to kiss me, I felt Reed's hands slide up my thighs, warming up my lower half.

I turned my head, freeing myself from Kane's kiss. "Stop. Please. I can't do this. We can't do this."

"Why, Lea? Don't you understand? Reed and I want to be with you. You don't have to choose."

How I wanted to believe him, but I knew it was impossible. "So you two have talked it over? You think this will work? No jealousy? For how long? I'm not trying to be difficult, but this isn't a Sophie Oak romance novel where one woman gets to enjoy the love of several men for the rest of her life. This is real. I'm flesh and blood and so are you. Sure, we might be able to fool ourselves and play house for a while, but what happens in a month, a year, or more? What guarantee can you give me that we have any chance at forever?"

Reed shook his head. "She sure does love to talk, Kane. We're going to have be on our toes dealing with her, don't you think?"

"Yes, that's for sure." Kane cradled my chin. "Listen to me. There's no guarantee, Lea. Not for us. Not for anyone. It's day by day. We're going to have really wonderful times together and we're going to have tough times, too. That's a promise. Will I get jealous of you and Reed sometimes? Likely. This isn't what any of us planned, but we're in it. I love you. Reed loves you. You love us. Reed is more than just my brother, my twin. He's my best friend. There isn't anyone else I could do this with other than him. Before you, he was my only family. Now, the three of us have the chance to become a family. I know it's fast and you have a million more questions, right?"

I had at least that many questions and more. "Yes, I do. If we take this to the next level and move in together—"

"That's happening this weekend, pet," Reed interrupted. "Kane and I have already discussed this."

They were really serious. "Oh my God. You two have figured this all out."

Kane smiled down at me. "Not everything. We'll do that together, Lea."

I was losing ground fast. Every argument I had would be flicked away by them easily. "What about kids?"

"We want a house full, sweetheart." Kane kissed me on the cheek. "Your mind is spinning. I think it's time to quiet that pretty little head of yours."

"Bro, there's only one way to convince her that this can work, and it's not talking to her until we're all blue in the face, if you get me."

Standing, Kane nodded. "Oh, I get you, bro."

"Let's show her. On your feet, sub," Reed commanded, leaving the bed and me behind.

My eyes popped wide. They meant to really *show* me. What if they were right that this could actually work?

Kane stared at me in a way that made me shiver. "Get out of your head, Lea."

"Did you not hear me, sub?" Reed's tone was more threatening than I'd ever heard it before.

It seemed to me that he and Kane had somehow traded their Dom demeanors. Reed was the tough, no frills one, and Kane was the more patient and tender one.

Reed leaned over me and pinched my nipples, causing them to sting and throb. "On. Your. Feet."

I snapped to attention, nearly leaping from the bed.

"Nice, Reed. Very nice." The pride and awe in Kane's voice was evident.

"We're going to use our tongues to make you suffer, sub." Reed shed his clothes, tossing them to the floor in a heap. Though I'd seen him naked before, I still couldn't get over how perfect his body was with its ripped muscles.

Kane undressed in front of me, too. He was well-built, one-hundred-percent male as well. "Pleasure can be its own type of punishment, Lea. You'll learn that tonight."

Their massive cocks were hard. My eyes popped wide. I'd been with each of them separately. What would it mean to move to the horizontal with both of them? I wasn't a virgin, but I also wasn't the most skilled person in the bedroom. What did they plan to do to me? My anxiety shook me. Would my fantasy become a complete disaster before it even got started?

"She's way in her head, Kane." Reed quickly stripped me of my clothes.

"I think we better get her out of her mind then." Kane knelt down in front of me. "We are in protocol, sub. Understand?"

"Yes, Sir."

"What state are you in?" Reed asked, kneeling down behind me.

I wasn't sure things could work like they hoped, but they were willing to try. I could at least let them. "Green, Sir. I'm green."

Reed parted my ass cheeks with his large hands.

I could feel Kane's hot breath on my pussy, amplifying my already hot desire. When he flicked his tongue on my clit, I was ablaze with cravings for more.

Reed began licking my backside, causing my insides to tingle and tighten.

Electricity pulsed through me, and my breathing turned to panting. I was dizzy and overwrought.

As my guys licked my most intimate flesh, the backs of my knees felt like jelly. Thankfully, Kane's hands tightened around the front of my thighs, and Reed's hands cupped my ass, holding me in place as they tortured me with their amazing tongues.

Each of their licks sent me higher and higher. The only thing left in me was need, overwhelming need. Logic fled my mind, as did my internal dialogue about all the reasons a life with them would never work.

Reed licked the tightness of my ass, filling me with utter abandon. My pussy was getting wet and my insides were clawing for release.

On and on, they brushed my pussy and ass with their tongues. I needed to grab something to try to hold on. My hands covered Kane's shaved head, and I pulled him in close and tight.

Reed's voice rumbled behind me. "Have you ever tried anal sex, sub?"

"No, Sir. Kane used a plug on me the night he trained me, but that's it." I thought about how boring sex had been before meeting them, and reveled in all they'd opened up for me.

"I'm glad. I want to be the first for you."

I closed my eyes, wiggling between them like a livewire. As Kane captured my clit between his teeth, a massive pulse shot through my body, and I screamed.

"That's my baby. Come for us." Reed's hands went up and down my back, giving me a delicious tickle that enhanced my orgasm.

Kane held on to my little bundle of nerves, delivering the perfect pressure that added to the sensations coursing through my body. My pussy's spasms came fast and hard, swamping me entirely. If they hadn't held me in place, I would've fallen to the floor straight away.

Kane release my clit. "Drown me with your sweet cream, little sub." Then he began lapping up my juices. His fingertips parted my folds, making me burn even more.

I felt something cold on my backside, and my whole body tensed. Reed tried to calm me. "It's just lubricant, sub. I'm getting your ass ready to take me."

Though I was still trembling from my orgasm, a bit of fear shot through me. "I-I'm nervous about anal, Sirs."

Kane stood and kissed me. "Don't be, sweetheart. We just both want to be inside you at the same time. It's the best way to make you really believe. Understand?"

"I'm trying to, Sir." Tremors shook me.

"Take a deep breath, Lea," Reed commanded from behind.

Kane nodded and smiled, reassuring me. I obeyed.

Reed sent one finger into my ass. The sting came and went quickly. He added another digit to the first, thrusting in and out of me. Soon, the pain was gone, leaving me with only intense need and desire. Nothing else mattered.

Kane leaned down to his discarded pants and pulled out two condoms from the front pocket. He tossed one to Reed. Mesmerized, I watched Kane rip the foil open and roll the condom down his shaft. I knew Reed was doing the same behind me.

"She's ready, bro," Reed stated.

Kane lifted me up. "Wrap your legs around my waist and your arms around my neck, little sub."

I complied, loving the feel of our naked bodies next to each other.

"Trust me, sweetheart. You only need to steady yourself. I'm the one holding you in place." Kane's tone was firm but also gentle. "Understand?"

"Yes, Sir."

He smiled and shifted me a bit so that my sex was touching the head of his cock. Another wave of heat shot through me as he lowered me down, piercing my pussy with his thick dick. Needy trembles rolled through me as he moved me up and down his cock.

I felt the tip of Reed's cock slide between the cheeks of my ass. I tensed at first, but as he gently rubbed my back, my anxiety washed away.

The tip of Reed's dick pressed on my backside entrance.

At that moment, I knew I had to have them both inside me. I wanted to surrender completely to these two Doms.

Reed commanded, "Take a deep breath, Lea."

I took in a huge amount of air.

"Let it out."

As I emptied my lungs of the last ounce, Reed sent his cock past my tightness and into my ass. The shock shook me, and tears streamed down my face. The pain and pressure was massive.

"Keep breathing, sweetheart," Kane instructed.

"You okay, Lea?" Reed asked from behind.

Unable to speak, I nodded. The pain was backing down fast, replaced by a new, powerful ache. Reed and Kane were inside my body, stretching, filling, and possessing me at the same time. Engulfed in the pleasure they were giving me, I felt more tears stream down my cheeks.

"You're doing great." Kane kissed me again. Together, they guided my body up and down, Kane's dick slamming in my pussy and Reed's cock shoving in my ass.

How long they continued pummeling me with their dicks I couldn't even venture to guess, but they continued thrusting, again and again, until my whole body undulated between them.

Reed's voice thundered behind me. "Do you like our cocks inside you, sub?"

"Y-yes, S-sir." My pussy clenched and my clit throbbed. I was right on the edge.

"Come for us, Lea," Kane commanded.

Every nerve ending fired hot and came alive inside me. My womb pulsed violently. Inside and out, a steamy turbulence shook me.

As Kane impaled my pussy on his dick one last time, I saw his eyes close. "Fuck! Grip me tight with your beautiful cunt, sub."

I clenched my pussy as hard as I could until I could feel the pulse of his heart from his dick.

"Yes. I'm coming, too." Reed growled behind me. "Hell, yes!"

Heat shot through me like exploding geysers. I wept like a baby, leaning my forehead on Kane's shoulder.

As Kane and Reed placed me on the bed and got on opposites sides of me, my thoughts quieted, replaced with real hope.

Reed touched my cheek, and I turned my head to him. "Did you remember that today is Valentine's Day?"

"It is, isn't it?"

"You're mine," he continued. "I love you, Lea. I don't just think it now. I know it."

"I love you, too," I confessed. He kissed me, and I melted into his lips.

When our kiss ended, Kane's hand cupped my chin, guiding me to face him. "I love you, little sub. With all my heart, I love you."

"I love you, too." His lips pressed into mine, washing me with pure satisfaction.

As we all drifted into much needed sleep, my mind quieted. I knew that this rollercoaster ride I'd gotten on wouldn't work for the faint of heart, but there wasn't any other place in the world I would rather be than between my guys, Reed and Kane.

Feb 19th

I am sitting in a chair enjoying some wine in my new home with my new dog at my feet.

How Beast survived the accident no one knows, not even the vet. The moment I walked into the house, Beast lumbered up to me and licked my hand, which surprised both Reed and Kane. Apparently, the dog has never been much of a people person. Before I moved in, my guys had decided to find a new home for Beast if he didn't warm up to me. I'm so glad he did. I can't imagine Beast not being here.

Reed and Kane have already gone to bed. They are beat. Serves them right. They insisted on carrying all my stuff: furniture, clothes, and boxes. I wasn't even allowed to unpack.

My job? Telling them where to place everything.

I love seeing my stuff mingled with Reed's and Kane's. On the far wall is a watercolor of Diamond Head in Oahu I had in my apartment. To the left of it is a dark bookshelf filled with tomes that my guys told me they have collected for years. My sofa. Their recliners. My dishes. Their silverware. And more. It's an eclectic style that works well.

Tomorrow night, Reed and Kane want to show me off in one of the most watched rooms at The Cell. It's set up like an Old West saloon. I would've never thought of myself as an exhibitionist before, but their intense pride in me is having an impact on my self-esteem in a very positive way.

I've never been happier.

We're actually going to have a future together. I know it.

God, I love them so much.

The End

MISTY'S BONDAGE DIARY

April 4th

6:15 p.m.

I got fired today, though the official terminology given from the impassionate Human Resources Vice President from the home office was "terminated as a result of a reduction in force." I am very familiar with the term, known in most circles around the company as a RIF or layoff.

I've been RIF'd.

I wish I could take back what I said to the hatchet man. "Thank you."

"Thank you?" What the hell was the matter with me? I should've pelted him with every expletive in my repertoire. Instead I smiled, picked up the package of doom he'd given me, and exited.

I already feel numb, disconnected, paralyzed even.

What to do next? That's going to have to wait until tomorrow. I'm exhausted. Need sleep.

April 6th

3:15 p.m.

On the couch, watching the Food Network. Just can't find the energy to do much. Tomorrow I'll get started revising my resume.

April 7th

11:52 p.m.

Tried to work on my resume but could never get past the first item—the personal statement. God, this is harder than I thought it would be. Time to go to bed and try again tomorrow.

April 11th

9:22 p.m.

I feel completely lost and unsettled. As you can see, I skipped a few days without writing any entries in this. I just didn't have anything to say. Since losing my job life has become so gray and empty, a void that I am not sure how to fill.

Tonight I'm going to enjoy the embrace of Mr. Sauvignon Blanc. Maybe he can help me get out of my head and actually relax me enough to get some real sleep.

April 12th

7:23 a.m.

Head hurts. I never drink alone and never like I did last night. Who would blame me after everything that's happened the last two weeks? No one. Not me for sure.

Glass of water, then back to bed.

11:45 a.m.

I've only been up for fifteen minutes. That's so weird. I've been waking up at five for so many years that I kept doing it even after I was fired. Not today. Not after all that has happened.

I just looked back at my entries. Nothing has really changed. Can't seem to cry, though I bet it's what I should do, what I need to do. It likely wouldn't change anything, but it definitely couldn't hurt. But how to invoke tears when they refuse to fall? My emotions seem distant, almost cut off from me. Everything is so dull, so flat, and so gray. Even the skies are filled with dingy, stone-colored clouds hiding the sun. Thank you, Mother Nature, for piling on top of my already leaden mood.

I'm not sure why I'm jotting any of this down here. Maybe I hope to make sense of some of this, sense of what I'm feeling—or should be feeling. Isn't that what a diary is for? Jotting down the happenings in one's life and noting how you are feeling? Who knows? I sure don't.

Mia bought this diary for me for my birthday, which was March 21st. Apparently, she and Lea are keeping journals and both say it has been fantastic for them. I smiled and thanked Mia for the gift. How could my life be so full of promise just two weeks ago? As I blew out the candles on my cake, I wished for the promotion I'd earned, the promotion I expected to be presented soon. Everything was in place. All the signs pointed to it coming. But it didn't. My birthday party seems like it happened ages ago, not three weeks.

Today, everything feels dark. Life has karate kicked me in the gut, chest, and teeth. All I've worked for has evaporated. I'm sinking and can't figure which way to swim to get to the surface.

Pity party, anyone?

God, I sound so morose.

I've begun this diary, my diary, on the wrong note. I guess the big question I should ask myself is "Who am I?"

Misty Gayle Weiss.

Daughter of Frank and Marilyn Weiss, and sister of Mia Weiss.

I'm thirty years old.

I earned my bachelor's in marketing from The University of Texas and my masters of business administration from Dartmouth.

I worked in a top-tier corporation specializing in telecommunications services for the past seven years until last week. I began as a data entry clerk and was promoted several times during my tenure there, finally landing the position of Executive Director of Public Relations, managing a staff of thirty-six in eleven states.

Damn. This is a diary, not my fucking resume.

According to Mia, I'm supposed to write down my experiences and most inner thoughts.

Let me start again.

Who am I?

A woman who is thirty years old, five six, size fourteen on good days, dark hair, green eyes...

Now I sound like I'm putting up a profile for one of those dating sites. What's wrong with me?

The truth is my job has been my whole world, my work demanding most of my attention.

I want—need—to see a couple of hundred messages marked urgent, a dozen e-mails demanding a return call, a line of people outside my office door with pressing matters that need my attention and skills. I yearn to have too much to do, all of it critical, and definitely not enough time to do it in. Then I would be back on familiar ground. Then this icy numbness would end.

Just two weeks ago, overwhelmed had been my reality, my life. Some might think that would be way too much to deal with, but it never was for me. I thrived when I had too many challenges, too many e-mails, too many deadlines, too many everything. With more time and absolutely nothing to do, what now?

Screw this. I'm going back to bed.

~

2:44 p.m.

I'VE STARED at this blank page for twenty minutes. I wrote this just to put something down. Maybe keeping a diary isn't going to work for me like it has for Mia and Lea.

~

4:44 p.m.

MIA CALLED to check on me. Lied and told her I was doing great. I'm just not in any frame of mind to talk to anyone, especially someone bent on cheering me up. Time to listen to some Guns N' Roses. Their songs are my go-to whenever I'm down. They can pull the tears out of me most of the time, and God knows, I need to cry or something.

~

MY COUSIN AND BEST FRIEND, Lea, called. Next I'm sure I'll hear from my two other cousins, her sisters, Ella and Amy, the latter of which is currently going by the nickname of Sunny, her choice.

God, Sunny? Really? It fits, but facing my gypsy cousin with her happy-go-lucky attitude might actually push me over the edge and into oblivion.

My family can't leave a person—me—alone. No. They have to prod and poke until I wave the white flag of surrender. I'm not normally the one to do that, but today I did. I agreed to go to Mia's party tonight, though I'm still thinking about blowing it off. What kind of company would I be?

"You need to get out, Misty. See some friendly faces. You'll meet some new people, too. Lex has some single guys from his club showing up. Kane and Reed know them and say they are okay."

"Lea, you think getting set up with some man is going to turn my life around after losing my job?"

"Might not turn your life around, Misty, but it could put a smile on your face."

I like to think I'm typical of a lot of women these days. For my gender there are two main paths to take in life, and many women can manage both quite well. Family. Career. Still, for most, they usually start with one of those choices, adding the other after the first is on track and unshakeable. How many times have you heard of the woman who takes a leave of absence from her corporate job to start a family for a couple of years or the other woman who leaves the kitchen table to jump into the rat race for her dream job?

Mia is a mile down the road on the family track, though she's still planning on opening up her counseling practice once she's finished her master's and certification hours.

I'm still dumbfounded how quickly she and Lex got wrapped up with each other. Actually, I'm not, when I think about it. Lex Brogan is a steamroller of a man, expecting anyone in his presence to stand at attention and salute. His demeanor sets the women's movement back a couple of decades. And that club he owns has got quite the reputation. I can't believe Mia and Lea are regulars with their guys at The Cell.

Lea Weiss? My cousin? Living with two guys?

God, I would've never thought she was capable of such. Jerry had seemed like the perfect fit for her. Not so. Apparently the twin hunks, Kane and Reed, share everything, including my cousin, and she doesn't mind. In fact, the last time I saw Lea, she illuminated the room with her smile.

Mia and Lea seem honestly happy. In fact, they seem happier than I've ever known them to be. Who am I to say what is right or wrong in *their* relationships?

Me? I took the path of career right after graduation, not to say I didn't consider the other, but that's another story for another time. I'm fine with that, really fine with that. I love my job. *Loved* my job. It was its own reward. I took great pride in what I did. Me and my team accomplished so much. Shit. Why can't I cry?

Tonight's event isn't actually a party. Lea called it a "munch." She and my sister are deeply into this kinky lifestyle, and apparently loving it.

"Lex and Mia are hosting this gathering for newbies like me," Lea said. "It's going to be super casual."

"Will people be talking about some of their experiences at Lex's club?" I asked.

"I'm sure they will, but there is no pressure. None."

"Will I be the only person not a member of The Cell?" That wasn't a position I wanted to be in.

"Mia told me there are several people coming who have never been to the club but are interested in learning more about it. So, honey, you won't be the only virgin. That make you feel better?"

Honestly, it did some. "I may not know my way around your kinky club, Lea, but I'm no virgin."

Her tone was gentle and kind. "I'm still discovering BDSM. I think both you and I will learn a lot about the lifestyle tonight."

～

8:48 p.m.

I ARRIVED at the party almost two hours late.

I stood in front of the massive home surrounded by every style of luxury car imaginable. They looked like jeweled accents by its three-story walls. My five-year-old BMW 328i looked like a little stepchild next to the shiny new Bentleys, Ferraris, Rolls-Royces, Aston Martins, and Lamborghinis. There were several models I didn't recognize but clearly weren't even in the realm of possibility on my salary—*correction, former salary*.

The reflection from the massive lit marble fountain in the center of the circular drive only added to the fairy-tale effect. Lex knew how to make an impact—that was for certain.

My little red Beemer had been a present to myself. Everyone, including my staff, peers, sister, and cousins, had been shocked at my most recent selection of transportation. It was flashier and sportier than my last car, a four-door previously-owned Honda Accord I'd driven for twelve years. I would've driven it longer but the repairs—engine, transmission, air conditioning, and more—would've cost more than the car was worth.

I'm not sure why I'd taken the leap away from my sedan norm. Impulse isn't my usual form. Would I be able to keep her now that I was unemployed? My gut clenched.

"No claim ticket?" I asked the guy in the tuxedo who had taken my key. I'd gone back and forth in my mind about going. Finally, I gave in after fifteen calls and even more texts from both Lea and Mia.

"No need. No man would be able to forget you." He smiled and his eyes fixed on mine, giving me a shiver. "Have fun. Your car is safe with me, miss."

"We'll see," I said, turning to head up the stairs to the double doors of my sister's new home. It looked more like a castle than a home in the suburbs of Dallas.

When I walked inside, the castle motif continued. Heavy wooden furniture was scattered around a foyer twice as big as my one-bedroom apartment. An elderly man in a butler's uniform greeted me. His accent was English.

"Welcome, Miss Weiss. Master Brogan and your sister will be pleased you have come. They are with the other guests in the music room, just past these stairs and to your right." The man was so formal. "May I escort you there?"

I had the oddest feeling I should curtsy or something, but instead I only said, "No thank you. I can hear the crowd from here. I'll find it on my own."

"As you wish, madam."

The whole place seemed odd for Lex's taste. I would've guessed him to be more on the modern side of things, and this home was anything but. The paintings I passed lining the walls were of land-scapes. Some looked like masterpieces from previous centuries, though I didn't recognize any of them. Classic sculptures, lit beautifully, were in alcoves.

I had no idea the sex club business was so lucrative. My sister lived here now as queen bee. Lucky girl.

As I entered the music room—more like a palatial ballroom—my jaw dropped to the floor. The space vibrated with the large crowd and the music from the four-person rock band playing on the stage oppo-site where I stood. Have you ever felt alone in a big crowd? That's how I was feeling, and nervous, too. I was wondering how the hell I was going to find my sister or cousin when someone tapped me on the shoulder. I turned and came face to face with two devastatingly hand-some men.

They towered over me, both several inches over six feet tall. The one to my left with the green eyes leaned into my ear and spoke loud enough for me to hear his deep rumble of a voice. "Are you Misty?"

I nodded sheepishly, admiring his thick, dark hair. He had the longest lashes I'd ever seen on a man. He wore jeans and a crisp white oxford shirt with the cuffs rolled up to his forearms. His hands were big and his wrists were thick. He was beautifully male.

The other man to my right, with the dark brown eyes and bulging muscles for days, pointed to his ears, indicating how loud the room was. He motioned for me to follow. The gray T-shirt he wore couldn't conceal the powerhouse arms and chest he had. Neither could the jeans hide his muscled legs, which were thick as a linebacker's. He turned and started walking toward a closed door to our left, giving me an unobstructed view of his backside. Michelangelo's David didn't have that nice of an ass.

Green eyes smiled as if to say everything was going to be okay. I wasn't so sure but didn't have a better idea at the moment. They knew who I was. Perhaps Lex or Mia had sent them to fetch me. I certainly hoped so since my heart was racing just being near them.

We left the hubbub and walked through a door into a side room.

"There you are," Mia said. She was sitting on a sofa next to our cousin.

"It's about time, girl." Lea patted the cushion next to her. Relief washed away my nervousness.

"Hey," I said.

Mia smiled. "Come sit with us."

Kane and Reed, Lea's men, were standing in the corner talking to three other guys.

"This is some party. Where's Lex?" I asked Mia.

"He's getting us some drinks. I see you've met Trip and Dominick." The corners of her lips curled up into a mischievous grin. Was she trying to play matchmaker? Which of these two studs did she have in mind for me? God, my sister could really push my buttons. I was in no mood to meet any guys tonight. I only wanted a distraction from my own thoughts about losing my job. I didn't want a date. But what better way to distract myself? Were these guys attached to Lex's club in some fashion? Likely. If so, I wasn't interested. Couldn't be. Mia and Lea might like the kinky stuff, but not me. I have had a few illicit dreams about the club after hearing stories from them. No. I had to remain focused.

I turned to green eyes. "Are you Trip or Dominick?"

"Trip," he said, fixing his stare on me, making my blood warm.

"Pleased to meet you," I said in my most corporate tone and held out my hand.

He took my hand in his and looked at my fingers as if they were made of priceless crystal. After several nervous seconds, his big eyes returned to mine.

My legs weakened and my breath became shallow. I wasn't about to make a fool of myself, so I steadied my stance and deliberately deepened my inhalation.

"The pleasure is mine, Misty. All mine."

Trip's good looks and pick-up lines were impacting my nerves. Hoping to gain some much-needed stability, I pulled my hand free and turned to the other handsome man.

"You are Dominick then?"

"The one and only. Call me Nick."

"Thank you both for bringing me to my sister."

"I'm with Trip on this one, Misty. Guiding you here has been a pleasure. If I have any say in this, and believe me I do, I will see you again."

I lowered my eyes to my fingertips as a fresh bout of anxiety rolled through me. Was he flirting with me? Was Trip, too?

When it comes to the nuances of attraction, and in particular how to communicate through the minefield of desire, I am always lost. Always.

The two delicious-looking studs just stood there staring at me. All eyes suddenly turned my direction. Were Trip and Nick waiting for me to say something? God, what could I say? What should I say? I remained mute for what seemed like several minutes but was likely more a few seconds. I opened my mouth to say something banal and was rescued when Lex walked into the room, distracting everyone away from me.

"Hey, baby." Lex placed a cocktail on the coffee table in front of Mia before lifting her up in his arms like she was made of air. Mia's man was quite strong. "This room is sure quiet. What gives?"

Mia leaned her head into his chest. "Your boys are teasing my sister, that's what."

Lex turned and glared at Trip and Nick. "This is a munch. Just a munch. Got it?"

Trip's left eyebrow shot up. "This isn't my first rodeo, boss."

"Mine either," Nick said. "We know the score. Doesn't mean we can't get to know this doll better." He pointed at me, and my cheeks burned like lava.

Trip nodded. "She's club bound, no doubt about it."

"Maybe so, but keep it casual." Lex looked at Mia. "Would you like to dance, sweetheart?"

"No, Sir. I'm going to stay close to my sister, if you don't mind."

"I don't mind at all, baby." Her man turned to me. "Misty, would you like a cocktail?"

"Vodka tonic, if you don't mind, Lex."

"Don't mind at all. Relax. This is about fun. You have nothing to worry about here."

I wasn't so sure as I glanced at Trip and Nick. They sure looked dangerous—*and inviting*.

Lex continued. "If you have questions about the club or the lifestyle, and I know you do, fire away anytime. Now or later."

"Later will be just fine."

Lex smiled like he knew something I didn't and left.

Trip and Nick excused themselves and walked over to Lea's guys and the other men.

"You okay?" Mia asked.

I nodded but the truth was I was far from okay. In fact, I felt like the world I'd known and been a part of, the world I'd impacted and made a difference in, the only world I knew, was crumbling into dust. Someone new was probably in my office by now.

I knew the drill well. "Reduction In Force" meant something much different than those three words. Lay off the well-paid and then bring in the cheaper worker bees. That was what RIF really meant. Whoever had my job now—likely a bright-eyed and bushy-tailed recent MBA graduate —would be paid half what I'd worked so hard to get. My long-time dream of reaching the top-tier executive level seemed like a fairy tale now.

"I'd like to say Trip and Nick are harmless, but they're not." Mia sipped her cocktail and glanced over at the two hunks I couldn't stop staring at. "They might be fun though, Misty."

"Not my cup of tea, sis. You know that." Mia and Lex were perfect for each other. That was very clear. Even Lea and her two men seemed suited to the unconventional relationship. But what kind of relationship would work for me? I had no idea.

"Why not?" Mia asked, fixing her unblinking eyes on me.

I shrugged. "Sex has to mean something to me. I know that's old fashioned, but it's true."

"Who says it wouldn't?"

"Stop treating me like you're my therapist and I'm your patient, okay?" But maybe tough love was exactly what I needed. My career was in the toilet. My love life had been virtually nonexistent. Why not have a wicked fling?

"What is holding you back?"

"Everything." Society for one. Lex's club might work for the fringe, but mainstream would never go for it. Then again, hadn't following the rules and doing what was expected been my whole life? What had that gotten me?

"Maybe it's time to take some risks, sis."

"Risks are one thing, but this...it's overwhelming." My heart started to race and my palms got clammy as I imagined what it might be like to be with Trip and Nick, *at the same time*. "You know this stuff. I haven't got a clue."

Mia put her arm around my shoulder, calming my nerves a little. "I'm still quite new to this life, Misty. Lex knows his shit and he's not about to put you with any trainers who aren't just as well versed in the protocols as he is. What most people don't understand outside the life is the subs in D/s relationships, whether 24/7 or just at the club, have their own power."

"I'm confused. The video you sent me was a lot to take in. I thought the woman, the submissive, was powerless."

Mia smirked. "You skimmed it, didn't you?"

I nodded my confession. Truthfully, when the couple undressed, I was burning on the inside. It might seem strange, but I've never watched porn before. Ever. Don't misunderstand me. I don't believe it is wrong, I just never have. Sure, I've been curious, but something always seemed to hinder me from enjoying it. What? I wasn't sure but could almost touch the invisible wall inside me that had been there for as long as I could remember.

"If you had watched all of it you would know that a submissive can say one word and everything comes to a screeching halt."

LEE SWIFT & KRIS COOK

"What are you two talking about?" Lex said, taking a seat next to Mia. "You look so serious."

"I feel serious," I said.

"This is a party, ladies." He waved to the two men whose very close proximity had tingles undulating through me.

I needed to play it cool or they would only have to crook their fingers and I would surrender everything. They bubbled over with sex appeal, and they'd made it quite clear they were attracted to me. To me? I glanced down at my designer dress and realized the packaging was so much better than what it was wrapped around. I needed to lose weight in the worst way. Long days at the office and grabbing whatever was close to sustain some semblance of fuel for my body had done it to me.

Why did they want to give me my first go at this strange and seductive lifestyle? To please Lex, of course. He was their boss.

But after talking to them awhile, I'm more than a little interested. I'm completely intrigued. I want to see where this could go. So I have a date. They are picking me up at 9:00 p.m. tomorrow night. Even if Trip and Nick might not be into me, I want to go through with it.

Whatever will I wear?

April 13th

2:16 a.m. – actually on the 14th, but my entry is about the 13th.

I'm in bed. How to begin to describe the amazing night I had with Nick and Trip?

It all started a little after 9:00 p.m.

I couldn't stop my hands from shaking. My reflection in the bathroom mirror worried me. Too much makeup? Not enough? God, how had I gotten myself into this mess? Two fucking hot Doms was how. My sister's manipulation was how. My desire to believe they might actually be into me, attracted to me, and not just agreeing to train me to please their boss, Mia's lover and owner of the club, was how.

But I needed this in the worst way, whatever their reasons. Since losing my job, I couldn't seem to find my footing, my balance. Everything seemed so off-kilter.

I glanced down at my outfit—number seven of the ones I'd tried on —and thought about changing. What did one wear to The Cell? I didn't have anything I would call sexy. Pretty, yes. Sexy, hell no. My curves didn't work in those kinds of clothes. So I'd done the best I could. Wranglers, my ropers, and a simple white cotton shirt had been my final choice, or so I'd thought. I glanced at the time on my cell.

The club's limo that Trip and Nick had arranged for me would be here any minute. *Crap!*

I stripped out of the clothes as fast as I could, leaving the Spanx on. I selected the simple black dress I'd tried on earlier, slipped into it, and went to the closet to select shoes. Shoes? For sex? Was I insane? The Doms had told me tonight's activities would be private and more talk than action. The talking part I could do, though each man's voice had already rumbled over my skin like a hot summer breeze making me uncomfortably wet. Was it too late to cancel, say I had come down with a flu of some kind? Female troubles? That usually worked to deter males from asking more questions. Yes, that would work. That's what I needed to do.

Wasn't that what I always did? The safe, sane thing? And here I was, between jobs, single and alone. So very alone. So many emotions whirled inside me, and I couldn't seem to sort them out. Why? Why did my own feelings elude me? Putting on my armor and playing a part was something I could do, something I always did. If they had an award for such a thing, I would have the trophies all around my apartment. Hell, my whole life had been one long act. It was exhausting.

No. Not this time. This time I was going for it, damn whatever consequences came. I put on my black stilettos.

Talk? Maybe we would just talk. But I believed Trip and Nick had other ideas. Would they be gentle? They sure didn't seem gentle to me. They seemed dangerous and so very delicious. A knock on the door told me my ride had arrived. I headed for the door. *Talk and action.* Time to discover what Mia and Lea had found. Would it speak to me, too? I wondered.

I looked through the peephole and saw Nick, wearing a chauffeur's uniform.

I opened the door. "Hello."

"Hello, sweetheart." His devastating smile made me weak in the knees.

"Where's Trip?"

"He is at the club getting our room set up for you."

Our room? I can still back out. It's not too late.

"Shall we?" he asked, offering his hand.

I took a deep breath and grabbed on to him, hoping to steady my suddenly wobbly legs.

Nick walked me down the sidewalk to the pearl white limo. The two college girls who lived in the apartment next to mine got out of their blue Mini Cooper.

He whispered. "Let's give them a show, Misty. What do you say?"

I nodded, thrilled to be on display.

As we passed the duo, he tipped his hat. Their cheeks turned bright pink. We walked down the sidewalk to the club's limo. I turned around and saw the young women gaping at me, wide-eyed.

Nick opened the door for me and I slid into the back of the car. The word *car* didn't quite fit to describe it. There was enough room for ten people in the passenger area. Another two could've sat with Nick in the front. It had a flat-screen TV, Blu-ray player, neon lights, and a privacy partition. There was a full wet bar with water, sodas, juices, and ice but no booze. I wasn't surprised. My sister had told me a few things about Lex's club. The limo was an extension of the club, being just one of several owned by it. The Cell didn't serve any alcohol. It was strictly forbidden. It might be a sex club, but they took their rules very seriously.

Part of me wanted to sit up front with Nick and another part wanted to stay put. I was nervous and excited at the same time.

"You need anything?" he asked, looking back at me when he got in the driver's seat.

"I'm fine. Thank you." God, Nick was so unbelievably sexy.

"You are quite fine, sweetheart. Quite fine, indeed." His words sent a shiver up and down my spine.

He pulled away from the curb and started toward the club. I looked out the window, seeing the streetlights on either side of the road. Was I really going through with this? Part of me wanted to. The other part —the part that had been my go-to for most of my life, the part that pushed me down the path of sensibility time and again, the part that never let me risk heartbreak—screamed at me to demand Nick take me back home. Every block closer to The Cell, doubt multiplied in my mind like a thousand spiders spinning sticky webs, each strand tugging at me to stop the trek forward.

I wanted to yell at him to hit the brakes and pull over. That would've been the logical thing to do. Wouldn't it? But wasn't my whole life just one long series of doing the rational thing? What had that gotten me? Right where I was—alone and jobless. Even though I was nervous about where Nick was taking me as well as what he and Trip had planned for me once I got there, I had to let go and latch onto something new. The gray of life was crushing me into nothingness. Would Nick and Trip change that for me tonight? It was a tall order, but I hoped so.

Thinking about what this evening might bring, I resisted. What was it going to bring? Although Mia and Lea had told me a little of what to expect, I really couldn't put my head around it.

The truth? I was a tad frightened. Few knew how paralyzed I could become by my own fear. It was the real reason I'd stayed away from the dating scene my whole life. In my job, I was in control. I had the power. Now, being laid off, I was adrift, out of control, powerless. In the oddest way, if felt good to give over the reins to others, to let Nick and Trip take charge. I didn't have to plan anything. They'd already done that. All I had to do was show up and let them guide me. That's what tonight was supposed to be about. I'd watched the film that Mia had given me. The safe word portion of the film put me at ease a little. Once we agreed on what it would be, Nick and Trip were supposed to obey it like it came from heaven itself. I could end everything by uttering that word.

As we turned the corner, I saw a long line of people standing in front of the club. Two giant, muscled men guarded the entrance. They were checking everyone's IDs, allowing only a few inside at a time.

"How long will it take us to get in?" I asked.

"Honey, you're a VIP. You go in through another entrance. There is no line there." He turned the limo down an alley, which was blocked by a giant gate. "All you need is the magic key." He punched something into an iPad. "Open sesame," he said with a laugh.

The gates parted, allowing us access. Nick drove up to a side door. A single man, who looked as big as his buddies at the front door, stood guarding this entrance.

Nick turned to me. "Here we are, sweetheart. Wait for me to open your door, understand?" His commanding, sexy tone made me tingle.

Was he already starting the training, making sure I knew my place tonight?

"I understand, Sir," I answered, recalling that was how I was to address him and Trip tonight according to the video.

He grinned, which made him look even more handsome than ever.

As he got out of the front seat, I took one more glance at my outfit. Had I chosen correctly? Would I stick out? Would he and Trip approve? I knew it was too late to change, so I tried to stop worrying about it.

Nick opened my door and offered me his hand. I gave it to him. Even that little touch seemed to send an electric spark through my body, but I thought it might've only been my nerves about going inside. Either way, the night promised to be something new and exciting.

I stepped out of the limo, and Nick led me to the VIP door. The big man working it didn't crack a smile. Dressed in a prison guard uniform, he looked terrifying to me.

Nick didn't address him, which surprised me. We walked through the door and into a reception room, which had plush sofas. At a desk was a woman who looked like the typical secretary I'd seen over my many years in corporate life, except for her attire. Her leather halter top and daisy duke shorts made me and my black mini dress appear more suited for a funeral.

"Hey, Nick," the woman said. "I've got Misty's paperwork all ready for your signatures."

Nick took the pages. "Thanks, puppy."

That was the oddest name I'd ever heard. Of course, I knew it had to be a nickname.

"Here you go." Nick handed the paperwork to me with a pen.

I felt a billion bees buzzing in my belly as my anxiety shot up. I already knew about the forms. They were part release of liability and part instructions about what was expected. Attached was a list of rules several pages long. I had been given a copy with the video.

My hand trembled slightly, which I hoped he and puppy didn't notice. Once I put my name on the forms, there would be no turning back.

"Everything okay? You did get copies of these already, didn't you?" Nick asked, his deep tone somehow reminding me of rich chocolate.

I nodded and signed the papers. "All done?"

"Almost, sweetheart." He took the pen from me and signed his name next to mine. "I'm the active member, Misty. You must have an escort once inside the main part of the club. You are my responsibility, mine and Trip's, for the rest of the evening."

I loved the sound of that.

"Here you go." Nick handed the forms to puppy.

"You're all set." The woman looked me in the eyes. "Trip and Nick have reserved one of my favorite rooms for you." She smiled. "You're going to have so much fun. Go on in." She reached under the desk, clearly hitting some kind of button.

A buzzing sound followed and Nick led me to the door, which was now unlocked.

We walked down one hallway with doors on either side, each having a number. Both Mia and Lea had told me about The Cell's theme rooms. What had Trip and Nick chosen for me? Puppy had said it was her favorite.

"Don't look any Doms in the eye, sweetheart. Keep your eyes on me only, understand?"

Just like the video had shown me. "Yes, Sir."

Nick led me down another hallway. We turned right into an open space that had a stage. There were a few members milling around.

"This looks more like a social event than a sex club, Sir."

"In about fifteen minutes, that will change. This is the public area for demonstrations, classes, and for Doms to put their subs on display."

My gut tightened. "I can't do that, Nick."

His face darkened. "What did you call me, sub?"

"I mean Sir."

"Better," he said, but his demeanor remained stern. "There's a demo starting soon that Trip and I want you to watch. You won't be up on stage tonight, but Sir Trip and I will decide what you can and can't do. Not you. Do you understand?"

I nodded. His male dominance swept over me like hot lava.

"Good. What's your safe word, sub?"

"I watched the video, Sir. I chose the traffic light colors."

"We'll start with that tonight, but after your lesson, Trip and I will help you choose your own personal safe words for next time."

I was shocked and thrilled that he was expecting there to be a next time.

"Here's our little present." Trip walked up, smiling broadly. He wore leather pants and a vest but no shirt, allowing me an eyeful of his very muscled chest. He had gorgeous ink on both arms that looked like barbed wire circling his bulging biceps.

Nick put his arm around me, making me warm all over. "She's a handful, buddy."

"Go change. I'll take it from here. You might make it back for the demo if you hurry."

"Deal."

I was vibrating from head to toe, and not a damn thing had really happened yet. My insides were jumbled up with desire as Trip led me to the seats right in front of one of the stages.

I thought sitting back a row or two would be less conspicuous. I already felt like a fish out of water. "Sir, could we change seats?"

Trip's gaze burned into me. "You don't decide where we sit. We tell you where to sit. Am I clear?"

I nodded, feeling heat rush to my cheeks. I was making mistakes and had only been inside the club for less than five minutes. I decided to try to take a deep breath before I opened my mouth again.

Trip smiled. "Baby, you're doing great. Don't worry. I wanted to sit you here to give you the best seat in the house. I don't want you to miss anything."

"Thank you, Sir." It was funny to me how tough and gentle he and Nick could be. Quite the combination.

We sat there as more of the members took seats around and behind us. Several people began setting up the stage. It was quite theatrical. Anywhere else, I would've thought I was about to see a play.

But I was at The Cell, Lex's club. This wasn't going to be some actors delivering lines they'd learned. This was going to be real. Very real.

By the time Nick got back and sat on the other side of me, the stage had been transformed into a strange looking place. It reminded me of a science fiction movie set—so alien with lots of flashing lights and displays.

"What do you think so far, sub?" Nick asked. "Quite impressive, yes?"

"Yes, Sir. My sister has told me about Lex's career in the film industry. It's obvious he's taken those skills and brought them here to The Cell."

"That's why his club is so popular, baby." Trip grabbed my hand and squeezed. "You should see the specialty rooms."

"Oh, she will, buddy."

Trip smiled at Nick's comment. "Absolutely, she will."

I was curious. "What is in those rooms, Sirs?"

Nick put his arm around my shoulder. "You don't want us to spoil the surprise."

A Dom walked onto the stage carrying a satchel and an ice chest. A woman who was wearing a silver collar and was dressed in a silver bikini followed him a few steps behind. He pointed to the floor by his boots. She instantly knelt down to that exact spot.

At first I found the whole thing strange. In this age, why would a woman want to be treated like a slave, a possession? When her Dom leaned down and whispered something only she could hear, I saw in her eyes something that I wanted in mine. Bliss. Happiness. Contentment.

I closed my eyes, afraid to see more.

Trip touched my shoulder.

I looked at him.

"Keep your eyes open and do not look away." The huskiness in his voice called to something deep inside me, something I'd felt from time to time but shoved down every chance I could. The corporate world would not suffer the weak, the submissive. I knew the rules. I'd conformed to what I had to become to survive. But here, at Lex's club,

I could be my true self. I would not only survive but I would also be liberated.

Now, I was sounding like my sister and cousin. I stifled a nervous giggle. This wasn't a spiritual journey with Trip and Nick as my guides. This was about sexual freedom. This was about fun. About release. About letting go. Nothing more. I didn't want to fool myself into believing it was.

The Dom placed the sub with her back to a six foot high silver metal cylinder that came out of the floor of the stage. He pulled her hands behind her and attached them to handcuffs that hung from the giant barrel.

I felt my heart speed up as the man palmed the woman's breasts with both his hands. He pulled out a pair of scissors that were holstered to his belt and snipped the straps of her top.

Electricity danced over my skin as the scene continued.

The Dom looked massive compared to the tiny sub. Shamelessly, he pinched the woman's nipples, standing to the side in a clear attempt to make sure everyone got a good look at his property.

Property? I wondered why that word had popped into my mind. It seemed archaic and outdated in this modern world. Women sat as equals at the tables of power and influence in this country.

Again, I looked into the woman's eyes and saw such joy it nearly overwhelmed me. Would I recognize her on the street? What did she do outside these walls? Where did she go? How did she live? She could be anyone. She might even be a high-powered executive, like I'd been just a short time ago.

Her Dom ran his tongue over her lips, and I felt myself licking my own. He caressed both breasts, and the moans that fell from his sub's mouth filled my ears like warm honey. I wanted to experience that kind of ecstasy.

Nick placed his hand on my leg and squeezed, causing my temperature to rise.

The Dom turned to those of us in the crowd gathered around. "I'm going to demonstrate various types of sensation play. I have found my sub responds well to being blindfolded during our sessions."

He smiled and brought out a blindfold, holding it up high for all to see.

I whispered to Nick and Trip, "Do you plan on using one on me, Sirs?"

Nick smiled. "Maybe, sweetheart. We have much in store for you tonight, but we don't want to spoil the surprises."

"Keep watching, sub." Trip grabbed my hand and brought it up to his lips. "We're going to learn a lot about each other tonight. We've learned much about you already just observing you watching them."

So much for having a poker face.

The Dom placed the blindfold on his sub. He bent down and opened the cooler. He brought out an ice cube and placed it on one of his sub's nipples. The woman shivered visibly, and I felt an empathy tremble for her roll through me. *Empathy? Or am I excited?*

I knew the answer was a little of both. What would I feel if I took her place?

The Dom dotted other parts of the woman's body with the ice. The sub had to be burning up because the first cube melted away quickly and her Dom had to bring out another one. I squirmed in my chair with every press of the frozen water to her skin. Tingles spread through me. I wanted to lower my eyes to get control of myself, but I'd been ordered to not look away. Why was I so willing to obey Trip and Nick? I wasn't sure but it definitely felt right. Was it being in this club where it was expected or was it something else that was inside me? Again, I already knew the answer, though it frightened me a little that I could be so compliant, so willing to surrender myself to them.

The man on stage smiled, pointing to his sub's budding nipples. The audience applauded their approval. He brought out a jar of honey and showed it to the crowd. He dipped his finger into the jar and dotted her nipples with the sweet nectar. Illuminated from the lights above the stage, the drops of gold glistened like jewels.

Without hesitation, the Dom began licking the honey off her breasts. His sub moaned and I felt my own throat begin to vibrate. I squeezed my legs together, trying to quell the pressure that was growing inside me.

Trip leaned over to me and began nuzzling my neck. Heat rolled through me. This was PDA taken to a level I'd never imagined. Nick fondled my breasts, causing my breathing to become labored. But I never looked away from the stage. I couldn't. I'd been commanded to keep watching, and that's what I meant to do. I would show them I could be good at this play, this game, this lifestyle—at least for tonight. I wanted to prove to them and to myself I was more than capable.

The Dom on stage brought out something I'd never seen before. "For those new to the club, this is a violet wand used in electric play, ladies and gentlemen."

Electric play? The levels of kink practiced at The Cell were beyond anything I'd ever imagined before.

"Dim the stage lights." The man was a showman. As the lights lowered, we all could see the dancing purple spark moving up and down the clear tube. He brought it to his sub's arm and a bolt jumped from the wand to her skin.

She jerked and I moved to the edge of my seat, feeling something electric dancing over my skin as well. I swallowed, trying to calm down. It didn't work. I was wired for more. I wanted to see more. I wanted to feel more.

The Dom continued demonstrating other kinds of sensation play with his sub. Although I was dealing with my worry about tonight, I still found myself imagining what it would feel like to be in the woman's shoes, up on the stage, exposed for everyone to see. My whirling thoughts revved me up into a state of overwhelming desire. I was hotter than I'd ever been before.

"Thank you." The man pointed to his sub. "A round of applause for Kim, if you please."

The crowd gave their approval.

I, too, applauded.

I couldn't take my eyes off of the woman on stage. Her tiny smile showed how satisfied and comfortable she was. No worries. Just bliss.

Completely entranced, I nearly jumped out of my seat when Nick squeezed my leg. I turned to him and could see the hungry passion in his dark eyes.

"The show is over, Misty. Time for the next phase of tonight's lesson."

"That's right," Trip said. "Demo is done. Time to put into practice what you've learned."

They both stood, each offering me a hand.

I gulped. Was I really going through with this? Again, my doubts resurfaced, causing me to hesitate for a split second. But then I glanced back at the woman with her Dom. The man was holding her close, holding her tenderly, holding her exactly the way I imagined it would be like to be held by Nick and Trip.

I took their hands and stood between them, still a little frightened, but my desire pushed me forward. "Lead the way, Sirs."

We walked out of the main area to a hallway with doors on either side. It was long and each step I took I could feel my heartbeat and breaths increasing. My legs felt weak like I had just finished a marathon. *But I must go on.* My intrigue had overcome my nervousness. Nick and Trip had made me watch the demo, obviously believing it would put me in a state of curiosity where I couldn't back out. They'd been right. Everything inside me, even my doubts, seemed to be pushing me forward to a new discovery. I wanted to learn about this lifestyle that had changed my sister and cousin. I wanted to learn more about Nick and Trip. I wanted to learn more about myself.

Nick grabbed the handle and opened the door. They led me inside. He shut the door and I watched him lock the deadbolt with a key, which he immediately put into his front pocket. A new tremble rolled through me. He and Trip were in control. I couldn't leave this room without that key, the key in *his* front pocket.

"What do you think of the room we picked out for you tonight, Misty?" Trip's question caused me to pause and look around the space.

It wasn't anything like I imagined it would be. "It looks like a high-end spa to me, Sirs."

"That a great description for it." Nick smiled. "It's called the Five-Star room."

No wonder. Off to the side was an overstuffed, comfy-looking sofa. In the middle of the room were two sunken tubs of water. One had steam rising from it. The other, clearly a cold tub, didn't. To the side was a massage table. Next to it were shelves that were loaded with creams and oils. Three of the walls were mirrored. White plush towels and robes hung from hooks against the far wall, which was painted a pale shade of lavender. There was even a glassed-in area, which I guessed was a steam room. On a table in the corner I noticed two black satchels, and the clothes that Nick had been in earlier folded next to them.

Satchels? I recalled that the Dom who had given the demonstration earlier had one, too. What was inside Trip and Nick's? My mind was spinning with a million possibilities.

"Sirs, there's something I need to tell you before we get started."

Nick and Trip turned to me, their sexy eyes locking in on mine.

"I'm not that experienced."

Nick smiled. "We know that, sweetheart. That's why we're here."

Trip added, "That's why Lex asked us to introduce you to the lifestyle. We have experience."

How many subs had they introduced to BDSM? I shoved that thought out of my mind, not wanting to dwell on that another second. "I'm not talking about BDSM, Sirs." I took a deep breath and blurted out, "I'm talking about sex. I've only been with two other men in my entire life, and I've definitely never had a ménage. The truth is I haven't had sex in a very long time."

They both smiled broadly.

"Honey, don't you worry about a thing." Trip grabbed my hand and squeezed. "We'll take things nice and slow."

"You're quite brave, baby." Nick began stroking my hair. "You are so sexy. You can't even imagine how thrilled I am to be your first introduction into the lifestyle."

They were being so sweet and kind. I felt my heart melt for them.

Trip walked over to the table and reached into one of the satchels. He pulled out a blindfold and a pair of handcuffs. "We'll start with these, sub."

I could feel my eyes widen, zeroing in on the two items that were clearly meant for me.

Moving his hands over my breasts, Nick whispered in my ear, "What state are you in?"

His fingers lightly pressed into my flesh through the fabric of my dress, warming up my body and making my nipples harden.

"Green, Sir," I answered, remembering the protocol for the evening. It was the truth. I was ready. I wanted to feel and experience this. I wanted them to be in control of everything.

Trip placed the blindfold over my eyes, and I felt a delicious tremble roll up and down my spine. I felt him unzip my dress, and removing it from my shoulders. He and Nick pulled it all the way off to my ankles.

"Honey, why are you wearing this?" Nick's fingers curled around the top of my Spanx.

"It squeezes me in places that need to be squeezed, Sirs."

"We'll determine if you need squeezing and we'll be the ones doing the squeezing." Nick laughed, which put me at ease. "For now, this ridiculous thing has got to go."

He and Trip helped me out of my Spanx. I was glad to have on the blindfold. It somehow softened the moment of them seeing me in only my bra and panties.

"My God, Trip. Take a look at this sub's gorgeous curves."

"I know. Her body is perfection in every way."

I couldn't believe what I was hearing. Whenever I looked into a mirror I didn't see perfection. I saw flaws, and plenty of them. But their words actually made me feel beautiful.

I could feel their hands moving over my body. Every touch brought out more tingles and warmth inside me. They removed my bra first. I felt them suck on my tits. In the darkness the blindfold created for me, visions of these two sexy Doms swirled in my head.

"Clasp your hands in front of you, sub," Trip commanded.

"Yes, Sir." I did as he instructed me.

I heard a click and felt the metallic coolness of the handcuffs locking my wrists in place. I could not see. I could not move my arms. I was at their mercy.

As they teethed my nipples into throbbing bits of flesh, I could feel my pussy begin to ache. Moisture pooled between my legs, and I began to squirm.

Nick licked my neck. "What state are you in, sub?"

"Green." My own voice seemed softer and more breathy than I'd ever remembered it being.

"Green?" His tone sharpened. "Is that all you have to say?"

"Really. I am green. I swear."

Trip laughed. "She's new, Nick. Time to remind her how she is to address us in play."

I felt both my nipples being pinched, delivering a wicked sting.

I instantly knew what I'd done wrong. "I'm sorry, Sirs. I forgot."

The pinch ended.

"Don't let it happen again, sub." Nick's lips feathered against my ear, causing a hot shiver to roll through me.

"Look at her thong, Nick. She's soaked."

I felt heat rush to my cheeks.

"Yes, she is."

I could feel their breaths on my thighs as they both knelt down in front of me. Even though I had the blindfold on, I couldn't help but tip my head down as if trying to see through the blackness at Nick and Trip, my two Dom teachers.

Their fingers moved up and down my legs, and I felt more liquid seep out of my pussy. I was burning up. I wanted more. But they were in control of what was happening. They were in charge of everything that was going on in this room. Whatever they willed, I was thrilled about all of it. This seemed so natural and freeing to me.

They removed my panties.

I started to squeeze my legs together but couldn't because Nick and Trip prevented me by holding them apart.

"I've got to touch this pretty little pussy." Trip threaded his fingers through my swollen folds, causing my clit to throb like mad. "I know I promised to go slow and easy with you tonight, sub, but God how I would enjoy moving this into high gear. I can't think of anything better than sending my cock into this sweet thing."

I wanted to scream as the pressure continued to build inside me.

"Damn your aroma is intoxicating, baby." Nick licked the inside of my thigh. "Your cream is delicious."

Vibrating from head to toe, I blurted out. "Green, Sirs."

They both laughed.

I giggled, knowing neither of them had asked about my state yet. "I thought you might want to know."

"She's perfect in every way, don't you think?" Nick asked Trip.

"Absolutely. Whatever you want to share with us from those pretty lips of yours, that's what we want. No. That's what we demand. Tell us everything. What you are feeling when we touch you like this." I felt his finger press on my clit.

"G-Green. So green."

Another hearty laugh from both of them sent me even higher.

"Let's put her on the table, Nick. And make her more comfortable."

"I agree. This is just an appetizer of what will come later."

Appetizer? A million ideas of what the main course might be spun in my mind.

They lifted me off the floor and carried me to the massage table. Lowering me down onto it, I was burning up for more from them. My body was on fire and needed release in the worst way.

They parted my legs wide. I felt something metallic clamp down on me, only this time it was around my ankles.

"This is a spreader, baby." Nick's tone was deepening with every syllable. "You won't be able to bring your legs together until it is removed. Understand?"

"Yes, Sir." I attempted to squeeze my legs together, testing the spreader. I didn't even gain a fraction of an inch. Just as Nick had told me, there was no way I would be able to make the thing budge. I was in handcuffs, blindfold, and now a spreader. I was Nick and Trip's student. I was theirs to do with as they pleased, and knowing that turned me on even more.

"Now we can get a really good look at this sub, Nick."

"I'm drinking all of her in with my eyes, buddy. I have to tell you I've never seen a more beautiful woman in my life."

"That's the truth. God, she's incredible." Trip kissed me, and I felt my toes curl. He removed the blindfold, and I looked up into his gorgeous eyes. "You're doing great, sub. Perfect."

"Thank you, Sir." I now realized that the blindfold, handcuffs, and spreader were only an introduction into BDSM. A few appetizers of sorts. What was the main course they had planned for me? Burning up inside like a volcano, I wondered if I would be able to take much more.

I was certain that I would explode if I didn't get some kind of release soon.

Nick and Trip, being Doms, most certainly could sense my state of suffering. And yet, they continued causing the pressure inside me to build with every whisper, caress, and kiss. It was maddening and wonderful at the same time.

Nick swirled his tongue on my abdomen while Trip sucked on my nipples. My pussy ached and my clit throbbed. I writhed in my restraints as they continued using their mouths expertly on my body, raising my need to a dizzying level.

"Please, Sirs. I need more."

"Yes, you do." Nick moved his hands down to my thighs and squeezed. "Much more."

He bent over and began licking and fingering my pussy. Crazed with want, I moaned and panted.

Trip covered my mouth with his, inhaling every one of my passionate outbursts.

I felt Nick's tongue circle my clit and his finger plunge into my channel.

"I can't hold back any longer, Sirs. I-I'm going to come."

"Drown me in your cream, baby." Nick captured my little bud between his lips.

My entire body erupted in a multitude of sensations that vibrated hot and electric. "Oh God. Yes."

Overcome by the incredible release, I felt liquid seep out of my pussy and could hear Nick lapping up every drop. Trip massaged my breasts and kissed me deeply, sending his tongue past my trembling lips.

As I continued shaking from the climax they'd given me, Nick removed the spreader and began massaging my ankles. Trip took off the handcuffs and rubbed my wrists.

Nick and Trip stepped back and removed their clothes. They were both pure muscle from head to toe. Each had ripped abs and bulging biceps. Unable to resist, I glanced down at their cocks, which were erect and massive.

Trip lifted me off the massage table as if I were light as a feather. I wrapped my arms around his neck and leaned my head into his chest.

He lowered me into the pool of warm water. He and Nick sat down in the tub, sandwiching me in between them. Even though I was quite comfortable from the heat of the water, I continued to shiver from the release. They massaged my shoulders, arms, and legs.

I felt like a princess being tended to by two noble knights. After several minutes, my shivers calmed down. Nick and Trip lifted me out of the water and dried me off with a heated plush towel. They lifted me back onto the massage table. I wondered if the lesson was going to continue and what was coming next. I didn't have to wait one second to find out.

They rubbed my entire body down with warm lotion that had an aroma of lavender. I had never been so relaxed in my entire life.

Nick stepped away as Trip continued caressing away all my troubles and tension.

Nick returned with a luxurious robe. "Sit up, baby."

"Yes, Sir." I swung my legs off the table and he placed it around me. It was unusually warm. I wondered how they'd been able to heat the towel and this robe.

"Feel good?" Trip asked.

I nodded. "It feels amazing."

He winked. "There's a hidden warmer near the back wall, baby."

Nick smiled. "We both knew you would like a little heat."

"I sure do, Sirs. Very much." I had never felt so cared for in my whole life.

Nick and Trip both dried off and dressed.

"Are we already finished, Sirs?"

"This was lesson one, baby," Nick said. "Time to talk through what you were feeling."

"Seriously, Sir?"

He grinned. "Yes, sub. Seriously. It's all part of it. That's what BDSM does. It opens you up to all kinds of things. Trip and I would be terrible teachers if we didn't talk to you about what you are feeling. That kind of discussion will help us to be even better for your next lesson."

A next lesson?

I couldn't believe how amazing this night had been. First, I'd learned that BDSM was about communication, both verbal and nonverbal. During our play, it had been mostly nonverbal. They seemed to be able to read my mind, touching me in all the right places. Second, they comforted me after my climax, putting my needs before their own. Every single detail was perfect in every way. And finally, and maybe even more importantly, there would be a next time. Another lesson with Nick and Trip.

"This is our room, Misty," Trip said. "Let's drop the protocols until we open the door and go out into the main rooms of the club."

He and Nick led me to the couch. I sat down in the middle. Trip sat next to me and Nick walked over to a tiny fridge and cabinet I hadn't noticed before. He opened the fridge and brought out a bottle of apple juice. He got a single glass out of the cabinet and filled it with the golden liquid.

He came back and sat down on the other side of me, handing me the glass. "For you, Misty."

"What about you two? Wouldn't you guys like a glass, too?"

Trip smiled. "We're more whiskey or beer kind of guys. Besides, this is all about you. Not us."

Nick placed his hand on my leg. "Speak freely, honey. Tell us how you're feeling about tonight and what happened? Every detail. Don't leave anything out."

I took a sip of the juice. It was deliciously sweet and refreshing. "I feel so completely relaxed and at ease. You both made me feel amazing. I never thought I was beautiful, or even desirable. But now, I realize I have a lot to offer. I discovered so many things about myself that I never knew even existed until now. I honestly don't understand how all of this could change me so much after only one lesson, but it did."

We talked for nearly an hour about everything that had occurred. They seemed to hang on my every word, asking me probing questions about how each thing we'd done had made me feel. I was so at ease with them, and sharing every detail seemed natural and right.

I had been so worried about losing my job, but this night with these two amazing Doms had given me hope again. My confidence was back. I felt empowered and strong. My future seemed bright.

Diary, Nick and Trip did nothing to satisfy their own hunger. They made this whole night about only me. If I'm not careful, I will lose my heart to them.

April 14th

I rolled out of bed late, stretching my arms over my head. I'd slept so well. Nick and Trip brought me home, kissed me at the door, and left with the promise of another lesson. Thinking about what their lesson might be made me tingly all over. I walked into the kitchen and made a pot of coffee.

My cell buzzed. "Hello."

"Good morning, sis. I couldn't wait any longer to talk to you. How did it go last night?" Mia had always been the more impatient one of us since we were kids. "I know it was wonderful but just how wonderful was it?"

"It was great."

"I know. I'll just come over." Mia's voice was interrupted by a beep. "Hold on. That's Lea on the other line. Let me click over."

I smiled, knowing our cousin was just as curious to learn about my night as Mia was.

Mia came back on the line. "Great news. Lea is free this morning, too. We're both coming over. We should be there in ten minutes."

"Come on. I already made coffee."

"Fantastic. See you in ten."

I poured myself a cup and sat down at my kitchen table. What to tell them? I knew they would grill me about every detail. It was their way, and I actually wanted to share all of it with them. I was bubbling over. My gloomy mood since being let go from my job had vanished into thin air, and all because of Nick and Trip. I grinned. Those two had been the perfect medicine to turn me around. I was ready to face whatever came my way. I believed I could conquer the world.

Taking a sip of my coffee, I looked out the window. The sun was shining brightly. I stood up, deciding to have this impromptu meeting with my sister and cousin on my patio. I cut up some fruit and toasted a couple of bagels.

The doorbell rang. *That was the fastest ten minutes in history.* I wondered if they'd actually been parked outside my door when they called me.

Opening the door and getting amazing hugs from both Mia and Lea, I noticed they were dressed to perfection. I was still in my PJs.

Each of them held shopping bags, which surprised me. "Did you two go shopping before you came over?"

Mia shook her head. "These are surprises for later. First, we want to hear all about last night."

"Okay." I led them to the patio. "Let's eat first. I'm starving."

"I bet you are," Lea said with a wink. "But since when can't we talk while we eat. Don't you dare think you can avoid telling us everything. I can see by your smile that you had a great time last night, didn't you?"

I decided I was going to be funny at first. "It all started with them painting my body with neon pink."

Mia's eyes widened. "What?"

"Yes, neon pink. Body paint. I painted Nick in blue and Trip in green."

They both laughed.

"Stop trying to pull our legs, Misty." Lea sipped her coffee. "Details. Now. From the beginning."

I told them about getting ready for the evening and all the outfits I'd tried on.

Mia nodded. "I completely understand. I did the same thing my first trip to The Cell."

"Me, too," Lea said. "When you're new, it's daunting to figure out what is appropriate or not."

"Would you believe I wore Spanx? That will never happen again."

"I bet Nick and Trip told you not to." Mia smiled. "Am I right?"

I shrugged. "They made me feel so beautiful and special. I had no idea how wonderful this lifestyle could be."

"Haven't we been telling you that for some time, Misty?" Lea grinned. "So you got ready. What happened next?"

I told them about the entire evening. We talked for nearly an hour, me giving details and them interjecting with their words of "we told you so" and giggles.

I leaned back in my chair. "You know, a woman could find herself falling for those two Doms quite easily."

Mia nodded. "Nick and Trip are two of the best trainers at the club. Everyone will be surprised when you take them off the market."

"Hold on, Mia. It was only one lesson."

"With the promise of another," Lea interjected. "It's a start. I bet they are into you, too."

My mind drifted back to the evening. "They gave me a climax that blew me away, but they didn't come. Why?" Doubt suddenly flooded my mind.

Mia grabbed my hand. "Hey. Relax. Doms have their reasons. You have to trust how they take you on this journey of discovery. Wait for lesson two."

Lea grabbed my other hand. "Absolutely."

"But what if I'm not their type?" I knew my heart was on the line already. I had feelings for Nick and Trip. "What if this is only about training me and nothing else?"

"Were their dicks hard?" Mia asked flatly.

Lea laughed. "Look at her cheeks, Mia. They are bright red. That tells me that those two Doms' cocks were hard as rocks, right?"

"So?" Recalling how massive their erections had been, I could feel the heat in my face.

"They're into you." Mia squeezed my hand and leaned forward.

"And I'm betting they will *be into you* in your next lesson even more, if you know what I mean."

We all three laughed and my doubts vanished.

"We brought you some things for your next visit to the club." Mia held up her bags.

Lea followed suit, holding up the bags she'd brought in with her. "And any one of these outfits we've chosen for you will get Nick and Trip's blood hot. Time for you to try some of these on."

I felt myself blush again. I really didn't know what to say.

Mia stood up. "Come on, Sis. You have to get used to dressing like this. Besides, you have the perfect body to pull any of them off nicely."

"Hardly perfect, Mia." I put my coffee cup down. "But I suppose you're both right. Time to push my boundaries. Let's see what you have for me."

Lea pulled out a black corset and handed it to me. The only other thing she gave me was a red pair of stilettos.

"Where's the rest of the outfit?"

"That's it," she answered with a grin. "Try it on."

"No panties or bra?"

Mia laughed. "Well, I actually got you a couple of thongs and some sexy bras to go with it."

She and Lea handed me all the bags.

I looked inside them and couldn't believe my eyes. "Do you really wear these kinds of things?"

"Oh," Lea said. "For about five minutes."

Mia nodded.

I could tell they were enjoying my embarrassment, but I decided I would show them. "Stay here. I'll be back for the fashion show."

I grabbed all the bags and headed into my bedroom. Emptying out the contents onto my bed, I picked up something made of leather that looked like several belts had been attached together. Its tag told me that it was a BDSM harness and on the back were instructions on how to wear it. "If they think for one minute that I'm going to march out in front of them in only this, they have another thing coming." I giggled. "I will put this over my PJs."

After I put it on, I looked at myself in the mirror and grinned.

Grabbing my bunny slippers that had been a gag gift from Mia last Christmas, I put them on and headed out to the patio.

I strutted out in my sexiest walk, hands on hips, breasts jutted out, and pouty lips.

Mia and Lea burst into a fit of laughter.

"I must get a picture," Mia said, bringing out her cell.

"Don't you dare, Sis."

"I dare."

"And so do I," Lea said.

They both snapped pictures of me before I had a chance to run. "Neither of you are leaving my house until you delete those pictures."

Once again, they burst out laughing.

"I guess the only question I have then is what's for dinner?"

The entire morning was such a joy. I actually did try on all the outfits and settled on one for my next lesson.

Hopefully Nick and Trip will call soon.

~

2:44 p.m.

AFTER MIA AND LEA LEFT, I filled my bathtub with warm water. I got in and closed my eyes, recalling last night and being in the hot tub with Nick and Trip. I let my mind wander and began to drift off.

I had a dream while I was in the tub. It was the best dream I've ever had. I've decided to put it here in my diary so I won't forget it.

I walked confidently onto the stage in my PJs and the harness. Nick and Trip were completely naked, painted blue and green.

The audience watching us seemed unaware of how odd we all looked. In fact, they were applauding.

"I feel like a giant smurf," Nick said.

Trip grinned. "And I feel like a Martian."

"What about me, Sirs? I'm here at the club in my PJs with a harness on top. That can't be right."

Nick shook his head. "You're not wearing PJs, baby."

I looked down and saw he was right. My pajamas had vanished, leaving me in only the harness Mia and Lea had bought me for this lesson.

Where had my PJs gone? I blinked and lifted my gaze back to my two Doms. The paint was gone. They were tanned to perfection, wearing Dom leathers that had my mouth watering. Each of them held a satchel and ice chest. I reached up and felt a collar around my neck. Once again, I looked down and saw my outfit had magically changed again. I was wearing a silver bikini, which I found odd since I didn't own a bikini, let alone a silver one. In the back of my mind, I remembered seeing another woman wearing one just like it.

Nick pointed to the floor by his boots. I knew exactly what to do and fell to my knees in front of him and Trip.

They began stroking my hair as they addressed our audience. I wasn't ashamed of being in front of all these people. My Doms saw me as beautiful, so I felt beautiful.

Trip leaned down and whispered, "Your ours, Misty. All ours."

I knew he was right. I was theirs and they were mine. My heart belonged to only them and no one else. Being with them was all I wanted. I felt so happy. I wanted to make them proud.

Nick and Trip placed me with my back to the six foot high silver metal cylinder. They handcuffed me and put the spreader between my legs. Heat rolled through me as they gently massaged my breasts, continuing to address our audience about what they were doing to me. I couldn't focus on their words, didn't need to. All I had to do, all I could do, was concentrate on their caresses.

Nick pulled out a pair of scissors and snipped the straps of my top. He and Trip pulled it down, revealing my breasts for the crowd, which roared with their approval.

I was unashamed of my body and happy to show it off. As long as my Doms were by my side, I felt safe and proud.

Nick and Trip began pinching my nipples, delivering sweet shivers throughout my body. I could feel the pressure begin to build inside me.

Both of them kissed me, one after another after another. Again and again. I licked my lips, which were beginning to swell and throb.

Nick held up a blindfold in front of my eyes. "This is for you, baby."

This felt so familiar to me. "Yes, Sir."

He placed it on me, and the darkness that followed felt so warm and wonderful.

I heard them open the ice chest. When they placed the cold cubes on my nipples, I moaned aloud, uncaring who heard my cries of ecstasy. As Nick and Trip ran the ice over other parts of my body, I felt my temperature rise. I was on fire. I wanted them more than anything. I didn't care who knew it. It was the truth.

The pressure continued to build as they lathered up my nipples with warm honey. When they began licking my breasts, I felt my pussy clench and my clit begin to ache.

I heard Nick address our audience. "For those new to the club, this is a violet wand used in electric play, ladies and gentlemen."

I squirmed in my restraints, excited and nervous of what was to come.

"Dim the stage lights," Trip said.

I felt the wand touch my arm and the electricity shot from its glass to my skin. I moaned again, feeling my pussy get so very wet.

Nick removed the blindfold. We were no longer on the stage. Now, we were in the room with the two pools—*our room*. He and Trip were naked, their ten-inch cocks out and hard as rocks. I reached for them, wrapping my fingers around their thick shafts.

"I need you, Sirs. I need you so very much."

"And we need you, baby." Nick lifted me into his arms and placed me back on the massage table. He crawled on top of me and plunged his cock into my pussy.

I clawed his shoulders and wrapped my legs around his waist, lost to my own need to be dominated by him and Trip. In and out. Over and over.

Without missing a beat, Trip took his place, filling my pussy just as Nick had done. This went on and on until I was screaming. I trembled violently as the pressure finally released and I came and came and came. Then Trip walked over and poured icy water on me. I was soaked and so very cold.

I awoke, splashing in the tub, my hands shoved down to my pussy. My bathwater was no longer warm.

It was the most erotic dream I've ever experienced in my life. Will I find the courage to get up on that stage in the real world? After only one lesson, Nick and Trip have changed so much for me, I have little doubt that a few more lessons will give me the courage to do more than I ever imagined, maybe even getting up on The Cell's main stage.

I guess I'll just have to wait and see.

~

8:47 p.m.

I LOOKED at all the outfits that Mia and Lea had bought for me that I'd spread out over my bed. My imagination went into overdrive with a ton of ideas for other kinds of sexy clothing. I had actually entered college hoping to become a clothing designer. I'd shoved that dream aside, settling on the degree I thought would be safer. Always my insecurities held me back. But I had sketched outfits from time to time as a hobby.

I opened the drawer where I kept my pencils and pad and began sketching out a few designs. When I finished, I smiled. They were really pretty good. I looked at the clock and saw I needed to hurry and get ready. Nick and Trip would be at my door soon. I put the pad away and chose the red mini dress. The tag said it was a size twelve. "That can't be right. I'm a fourteen." But I'd tried it on earlier and it had fit perfectly. "It's got to be tagged incorrectly."

It fit this morning, so I decided to put it on again. Besides, it was the least scandalous of the lot my sister and cousin had brought me.

"Baby steps." Mia wasn't here, but I felt like I needed to voice the reason for my choice aloud. "This is only my second lesson."

I imagined what my sister would say. "At least wear some sexy underwear, Misty."

"Fine," I said aloud again. Then I laughed, knowing I was being ridiculous arguing with my sister who was several blocks away at her own home with her own Dom.

I selected the sexiest thong and bra on the bed. Then I decided I would spice up my choice by wearing lacy stockings, hoping Nick and Trip would like them.

I wore the red stilettos that were at least an inch higher than any in my closet. "Like Lea said, if I'm lucky, I'll only have them on for five minutes." I laughed.

After I finished putting on everything, I took a last look at my reflection in the mirror. I wore my hair hanging loosely to my shoulders, just the way my sister and cousin had suggested I wear it. I wasn't disappointed in the way I looked for the first time in my life. I actually looked pretty and sexy. "Maybe I am a size twelve."

The doorbell rang. I went and answered the door.

Nick and Trip stood there side by side, already wearing their Dom gear. Damn, they were sexy beasts. They both looked me up and down with smiles and their eyes beaming.

"My God, you look gorgeous, Misty." Nick pulled me into his arms. Even in the heels, I had to tilt my head to look into his eyes. He devoured my lips, causing my heart to race. When he released me, he turned me to face Trip.

"You are stunning, baby." Trip pressed his mouth to mine, tracing my lips with his tongue. My legs became wobbly, but his arms around me kept me steady.

"You made me feel so good. I'd like to do this again."

"What do you mean?" Nick asked.

"You'll see." I stepped back into my home and shut the door.

I could hear them laughing. Then the doorbell rang.

I grinned and opened the door. "Hello, you handsome devils."

They repeated the kisses and compliments, increasing my tingles.

I guess I really am a size 12.

"Time to go, sweetheart." Trip grabbed my hand and he and Nick led me to the limo parked on the street. It was different than the one I'd ridden in for my first lesson. This one wasn't from The Cell, which I found odd. Did the club lease other limos on busier nights? I imagined the place would be packed with members this evening. When we got close to the vehicle, a man got out of the driver's seat and came around and opened the door.

I turned to Nick. "You're not driving?"

"I've got better things to do tonight, baby," he said with a grin.

I got into the limo and Nick slid in next to me. Trip came around the other side. Once again, I was between them, just where I loved being.

I was glad there was a privacy partition between the driver and us. The vehicle could seat at least twelve more passengers. "This is bigger than the other limo."

Nick nodded, reaching into the mini fridge. "Would you like a glass of wine, baby?"

"Yes, but isn't that against the club's rules?"

They both shrugged.

"Come on, guys. A different limo. A glass of wine. What's going on?"

Trip put his arm around my shoulders. "It's a surprise for you."

"A surprise? What about my lesson?"

Nick handed me a glass of white wine. "This is about your lesson, Misty."

Trip smiled. "Just sit back, relax, and enjoy."

I took a sip of the wine. "Yes, Sirs. I have to admit I'm very intrigued about all of this."

Nick touched my cheek, giving me a nice little tingle. "We knew you would be."

After I finished my wine, Trip placed his hand on my thigh just below the hem of my dress. He moved his fingers up my thighs and under the fabric, sending a sweet shock up and down my body.

"Baby, I'm tired of trying to imagine what you have on under this dress." Trip's hand reached my thong, and he pulled it down to my ankles.

Heat flooded my cheeks and my eyes darted to the partition. The driver couldn't see anything, but still I felt so naughty and excited at the same time.

Trip lifted my legs and removed my thong completely. He smiled and tucked it into his pocket like a trophy. I knew I was never getting it back from him.

Nick grabbed me by the back of my neck and pulled me in for a deep kiss. His tongue demanded entrance, and I parted my lips, surrendering to his dominance. Trip touched my pussy lightly, making me warm for the promise of what was to come.

The entire drive, they continued kissing and caressing me until I was vibrating from head to toe. When the limo finally came to a stop, my lips were swollen and my skin was covered in goose bumps.

I looked out the window and was surprised. Iron gates were swinging open to a gorgeous estate. "This isn't the club."

Nick grinned. "True. It isn't the club."

We rode down the long, tree-lined drive to the front of the two-story mansion. It had an Old World elegance. "Where are we?"

Trip opened the limo door and stepped out, offering me his hand. "Our house, baby. It's our final destination this evening."

I took Trip's hand and exited the limo. "Your house? Seriously?"

Nick came around from the other side, joining us. "Yes, seriously. You like it?"

"Like it? Oh my God, Nick. It's incredible. I feel like Cinderella arriving at the ball." Still holding Trip's hand, I grabbed Nick's. "Except instead of one prince I get two."

I was thrilled they had brought me to their home but also a little nervous. *Why have they brought me here?*

"Will that be all?" the driver asked, startling me.

I'd been so mesmerized by the drive and seeing their house, I'd forgotten he was still there.

"Yes, Charles. That will be all."

The man nodded and got back into the limo.

After he drove off, I let my eyes wander over the beautiful mansion and manicured lawn. "You both live here?"

"I live in the right wing and Trip lives in the left wing."

I giggled. "I've never been in a home with wings before."

Trip smiled. "Time for you to experience that, baby. Let's give you a tour."

He and Nick led me into their house. When the double doors opened to the opulent foyer, I nearly fell over. There was a winding wooden staircase and marble floors. The furnishings were plush and the art on the walls was stunning.

Though I was shocked at their obvious wealth, I wasn't about to ask how they'd come to it or why Nick drove a limo for the club. It was none of my business.

Nick laughed. "Look at her, Trip. Our little sub's head is spinning with a ton of questions."

"I can see that." Trip walked me over to a large portrait of a very distinguished looking man and woman. "These are our grandparents, Misty. My paternal grandparents and Nick's maternal. Nick and I are cousins."

"You are? I had no idea." I looked in both their faces and could see the resemblance to the couple. Trip looked a lot like his grandfather and Nick had his grandmother's bright eyes. Turning to them, I laughed. "I would've never taken you for trust fund babies, guys."

Nick put his arm around my shoulders. "Far from it. Our family is about everyone making it on their own, baby. Trip and I started a retail business of department stores when we were in our early twenties."

"Have you ever heard of Lussos?"

I was floored. Lussos was a top-tier department store, like Niemann-Marcus and Barneys, catering to the rich and famous. "Of course I have. Back in my corporate job, I worked with some of the buyers for your company. Aren't there are over a hundred locations in the United States?"

With his eyes full of pride, Trip smiled. "Actually we're approaching two hundred here in the States, with ten more in Canada and twelve in the U.K."

"Does Lex know?" I asked, thinking about Nick driving the limo.

The both nodded.

"What about Mia?"

"Only Lex, sweetheart." Trip stroked my hair. "No one else at the club knows."

"Baby, we like to keep our business side and personal life separate." Nick kissed my forehead.

I was thrilled that they trusted me enough to bring me here.

The showed me the rest of their home which could've been featured in a magazine. It suited them both. Eclectic and masculine. They walked me to a balcony that looked out to a massive pool and more manicured grounds that went on as far as the eye could see. "Amazing."

"You approve?" Trip asked, his arm around my shoulders.

"Of course I approve." I leaned my head into his chest. I still couldn't believe these two Doms, my trainers, were the owners of Lussos. It was so surreal.

"One more thing to show you, baby." Nick brought out a key.

They led me down the stairs to a door off the kitchen. I hadn't noticed it before.

Nick inserted the key into the lock. "And now for the real surprise. Mine and Trip's private dungeon."

I walked through the door into a room that was expansive, filled with all kinds of contraptions and a wide variety of sex toys. Some I recognized but others were new to me. My heartbeat shot up, as did my temperature.

"Lesson two, sub," Trip's voice returned to that commanding tone he'd used on me when we'd been at the club.

"Yes, Sir."

Trip led me to a leather bench. "Sit."

I sat down.

"Do not move."

"Yes, Sir."

He and Nick started pulling out all kinds of toys and devices.

I was so excited about my second lesson. I wanted to try everything.

Nick held a pair of handcuffs and a blindfold, which I had already experienced. I saw Trip grabbing items I was not familiar with. One of them looked like a chain of some sort. Another reminded me of the electric toy I'd seen at the club. The Dom from the other night had used something like it up on the stage with his sub, but the one in Trip's hand was thicker and longer.

"Let's start our sweet silk out on the St. Andrew's Cross, Nick."

They'd chosen *silk* as my scene name when we'd talked the night before. The word made me feel special and beautiful. Silk was soft to the touch and yet was very durable.

"I agree."

They went over to one of the contraptions. It looked like a giant *X* attached to a black metal base. There were cuffs for hands and ankles at each end. The pulled it out into the center of the room. I could tell it was quite heavy and stable by the effort it took them to move it. Nick and Trip were strong men, so I knew the cross must have been several hundred pounds.

They continued setting up the room for my lesson. Pulling side tables next to the big *X*, their meticulousness gave me comfort. They took this very seriously, and that made me trust them even more.

"Time to play, silk." Nick motioned me over.

"Yes, Sir." I stood in front of them.

Trip cupped my chin. "We're going to step things up tonight. Did you come up with new safe words, baby?"

I nodded. "Yes, Sir. I thought we could use *yummy* to let you know you're rocking my world. *Spicy* could let you know I'm getting close to a hard edge. And *sour* could be my hard stop word."

They both smiled.

"Those are great choices, silk." Trip smiled, filling me with pride. I'd done well.

He and Nick repeated the words back to me with what each meant, making certain that we all were in agreement.

"We'll be checking in with you about your state. The only thing we want from you is to let us know how you're feeling. Understand?"

"Yes, Sir."

Nick stepped back, his hot gaze locking on me like a vise. "Strip, sub."

His sudden command shocked me and I hesitated. I'm not sure why. I wanted all they were clearly offering me.

"Bad girl, silk. I gave you a direct order. What are you waiting for?"

"Nothing, Sir. I'm sorry."

"You will be, but that will be part of the fun. Now, strip. Give Trip and me a great show." Nick turned on some music, which had a deep, thundering beat that vibrated along my skin.

I knew all I had was my shoes, dress, and a bra. My thong was still tucked away in Trip's pocket. I started by pulling the knit dress from my shoulders, and as seductively as I could, I slowly moved it down my body. Even though my heart was racing, I was enjoying myself. I wasn't Misty in here, a woman who had lost her job, a woman full of inhibitions, a woman who struggled letting go. In here, in Nick and Trip's private dungeon, I was silk, a sub who was free and full of excitement, wanting to please her Doms.

I looked at Nick and Trip and saw the bulges in their leather pants and the heat in their eyes and knew I was turning them on.

I giggled and ran my hands all over my body, releasing the bra. Without thinking, I threw it at them. Then I stopped. "Oh God. I'm sorry, Sirs."

They both laughed.

Nick grinned. "You will pay for that, baby. Your bottom will be nice and pink when we're done with you."

I bent down to remove my stilettos.

"Not your heels, silk." Trip placed his hand on my shoulder. "Leave them on for now." He kissed me. "You did good. That was quite the show you gave."

"Thank you, Sir." What was it about him and Nick that gave me such tingles? They were strong and in control, yet they could be gentle and sweet. I felt my heart warm with every word, every look, every touch they gave me.

Without a word, they turned me around and moved me to the St. Andrew's Cross. They attached me to it face first, leaving my naked backside totally exposed. They cuffed my wrists and ankles. My heart skipped several beats as my excitement grew.

I licked my lips, wantonness causing droplets of moisture to pop up on my skin.

"Silk, your hesitation to my command to strip earned you five smacks on this lovely ass." Nick's hands cupped my cheeks. "Understand?"

"I do." I gulped, seeing Trip out of the corner of my eye picking up a big paddle. Was that what they planned on using on me.

"Is that all you're going to say, sub? How are you supposed to address Trip and I when we're in play?"

Oh God. I screwed up already. "I do, Sir. I'm so sorry, Sir. I-I'm nervous."

He kissed me on the back of the neck. "Of course you're nervous. That's all part of the scene, sweetheart. Still, you must learn. Five more smacks for a total of ten."

I couldn't help but grin. This was a game. I wanted them to know I was up to this. I wanted to make them proud. "I can take more, Sir."

"That's not your call, silk. That's ours. Still, I'll enjoy making your backside red. We'll start with ten and see if you need more."

Trip held up the paddle in front of my eyes. "What state are you in, silk?"

"Yummy, Sir."

He winked and moved behind me. "Ready?"

I closed my eyes, bracing for the impact of the toy. "Yes, Sir. I'm ready."

In a split second, I felt the slap of the paddle flatten out my ass. It burned deliciously and my whole body heated up.

"You were very bad, silk." Another slap of the paddle delivered a fresh sting to my left cheek.

I was getting tingles in my pussy, and my clit began to ache. How was that possible from getting a spanking? I didn't understand but I liked it.

Three more slaps from Trip had me vibrating from head to toe. I writhed on the cross, unable to stop shaking.

"How many more, sub?" Nick asked. "Give me the count."

My head was spinning. "Five, Sir. Five more."

He tugged on my hair. "Very good. Five. If you prove to me you can take it, maybe you'll get a couple more." He ran his hand down my sides and reached around me until his fingers were touching my pussy and clit. "We'll see. Trip, she's so wet. I think silk likes being punished. Hand me that paddle."

Nick's smacks came one right after the other. Five slaps landed on every part of my ass. My eyes welled up and my pussy got even wetter.

Nick leaned in, feathering his lips against my ear. "Are you going to be a good girl from now on, silk?"

"Yes, Sir. I-I promise."

Nick began applying lubricant to my ass. I tensed. I'd never had anal sex before.

"What state are you in, sub?" Trip asked.

I thought about fudging the truth but was certain they would sense it. "Spicy, Sir."

Nick's fingers stopped slicking up my anus. He kissed the small of my back. "It's okay, baby."

Trip stroked my hair. "Nice and slow, silk. Take a deep breath."

Their loving touches and words eased my sudden bout of worry. I let out a long, satisfying breath.

Nick cupped my ass tenderly. "What state are you in now, baby?"

"Yummy, Sir."

"What about when I do this?" He circled my anus with his lubed up finger, sending a tremor through my whole body.

Even though I'd never had anal sex before, I trusted them. "Yummy, Sir."

They'd sworn to stop if I called out my safe word. Everything was going to be wonderful. They'd proven over and over that they knew what I would respond to better than I did myself.

"And when I do this?" He sent his finger in and out of my ass, causing a renewed heat to wash over me.

"Yummy, Sir. Yummy. Yummy."

They both laughed again, which was music to my ears.

The pressure inside me grew and grew. I wanted more, needed more.

"Listen to me carefully, sub." Nick's voice thundered from deep within his chest. "This is only your second time, but you are doing so great. You're a natural. We want to push your limits some. I'm going to put a plug inside this pretty ass. You're so tight. You've never had anal sex before, have you?"

"No, Sir," I admitted.

"Damn, that's great." His words thrilled me. "Virgin ass, Trip."

"I heard. Silk, how are you doing?"

"Yummy, Sir."

Nick continued finger-fucking my ass, and I knew I wanted them to be my firsts.

"We need to get you ready for our cocks, baby," Nick said. "This plug will help with that."

I felt him trace my back with something rubbery.

More lubricant and another finger had me moaning like mad.

"Take a deep breath for us, silk," Trip commanded.

I did.

"Let it out nice and slow."

Again, I obeyed instantly.

When the last bit of air left my lips, I felt Trip's hand on my pussy and clit. Then Nick plunged the toy into my ass, stretching me wide. Gasping, I felt every inch of the plug. Pain and pleasure created a potent combination that caused the pressure inside me to multiply and expand.

Dizzy with desire, heat flooded every part of my body. My pussy got even wetter. I'd never felt this way before. I never even knew it was possible before. But here I was, in Nick and Trip's private dungeon on their St. Andrew's Cross, with my ass burning from the paddling, with the plug stretching me wide, and with their hands caressing me lovingly, more turned on than I'd ever been in my entire life.

"I just love this, Sirs. Yummy. Yummy. Yummy."

They rewarded me with lusty laughs, which I would never tire of hearing.

"Squeeze on the toy, silk." Nick kissed the small of my back again, sending a delicious shiver up and down my spine. "Close your eyes and concentrate on what your body is responding to. Tell us everything."

"Yes, Sir. The little bit of pain I felt from the plug when you first put it inside me is completely gone. All I feel now is an overwhelming need."

"A need for what, silk?" Trip asked, his words deep and dangerous. "Don't hold back."

"Yes, Sir. I-I need you inside me. I need both of you, Sir. I'll go mad if you don't make love to me soon."

"God, you're something special, baby." Nick removed the cuffs around my ankles.

"That's for sure." Trip uncuffed my wrists.

They rubbed my arms and legs, which were stinging slightly and completely weak from being restrained. They set me back on the bench. The plug moved deeper into my ass, giving me a nice jolt.

Nick and Trip shucked their leathers, tossing them to the side. They both rolled condoms down their long erect cocks. I couldn't wait to feel them inside my body.

Trip lifted me off the bench and into his arms. I wrapped my hands around his neck and my legs around his waist.

"I'm going to remove the plug, baby."

When the toy was out of my ass, my desire shot up like crazy. "Please, Sirs. Please. I need you."

"You've earned it, silk." Trip's eyes swam with hunger. "Every bit of our big cocks."

Holding me against him, he lowered my body onto his dick.

I panted as he pierced my pussy inch by inch. "Yes. Yes. Yes."

Several strokes from Trip scrapped against that perfect spot, adding to my suffering.

I felt Nick move behind me. He parted my ass cheeks with his hands and I could feel the head of his cock touching my tightness. "Deep breath, sub."

I obeyed.

"Let it out."

I blew it out as fast as I could. Nick shoved his cock into my ass, stretching me much more than the toy had.

I'd never felt so filled, so complete, so dominated. They were claiming my body. I was theirs. I was *silk*.

They plunged into me in synchronized thrusts. Again and again. Over and over.

Nick reached around me and pressed on my clit.

I screamed as sweet release erupted throughout my body. Every cell exploded to life. Every nerve vibrated with electricity. My heart thudded hard in my chest. My breaths came fast, but still I needed more oxygen. I was deliciously dizzy and loving every second of it.

I clenched on their cocks with my body, Trip in my pussy and Nick in my ass.

They shoved hard into me and both stiffened followed by climatic groans.

I could feel their dicks pulsing inside me as a flood of sensations swamped me utterly.

I writhed between them for several minutes, riding out every trembling moment of the climax they'd given me. Tears of relief soaked my cheeks as they carried me out of the playroom to one of the many bathrooms in the house. Without a word, they walked into the massive shower, which was big enough for the three of us. Nick turned on the water. It was warm and felt incredible on my skin.

I was totally spent, but that didn't matter. They washed me, cleaning me with their soapy hands. Trip even shampooed my hair.

I felt like a princess.

When we were all cleaned, they helped me out of the shower and dried me off. I was not allowed to give them any assistance whatsoever. They were in charge. They were in control. They were Doms, through and through, and I loved every second of it.

They carried me to a big bed, where they placed me between them. I'd never felt more relaxed in my whole life.

We just lay there and drifted off to sleep.

April 15th

8:08 a.m.

I awoke to the sun coming through a window. I wondered how long we'd been sleeping. I hadn't planned on spending the night, but clearly I had. This lifestyle was giving me the best sleep I'd ever experienced. After my first lesson, I had slept like a baby. This second lesson had knocked me out completely. I hadn't stirred any the entire night.

As long as I was in training with Nick and Trip, there would be no need for sleeping pills for me.

I sat up, realizing I was alone. Where were Nick and Trip? Then I smelled fresh brewed coffee. I smiled. My life had definitely gone a completely new direction. Nick and Trip were at the center of this change.

I knew I was falling too fast and too hard for them, but no matter how hard I tried to keep my heart in check, my feelings continued to grow and grow. The things they'd already done for me were amazing. How could any woman not fall in love with two handsome Doms like them?

Doms. I reminded myself that was what they were to me. Training Doms. Nothing more.

"Hey, sleepy head." Nick came in with a pot of coffee and three cups. He handed one to me. Trip followed him into the room carrying a tray of breakfast goodies.

I swung my feet off the bed, imagining all the subs they'd trained at the club. There likely were several dozen, maybe more. "Thank you. How long have you two been awake?"

"About an hour," Nick said, taking a seat next to me on the bed. "Did you sleep well, sweetheart?"

I nodded, taking a sip of the coffee. "Perfect. Thank you." Was I only a student to introduce into the lifestyle to them?

Trip took a seat on the other side of me and kissed me on the cheek. "My God, Misty. You wake up so beautiful in the morning. What's your secret?"

I grinned. "Sleeping between two gorgeous men, that's what."

What if I was wrong? What if they were really into me? I recalled last night and how tender they'd been with me, especially in the shower. I'd never felt more pampered or cared for ever.

Was I only fooling myself? Maybe, but maybe not.

"You did great on your second lesson, baby." Trip grabbed my hand and squeezed. "More to come. Nick and I plan on taking you back to the club tonight for lesson three."

"You're going to love what we have in store for you," Nick said. "It won't be long before you'll be ready to take center stage just like that sub you saw the other night."

Even though my gut twisted into a knot, I still kept a smile on my face. "Will that be my graduation into the life?"

Nick put his arm around me. "That's one way of looking at it."

I needed to remember they were training me, and they were the best. Mia had told me so. I knew my heart was going to break apart, but I was still glad there was the promise of more lessons to come. "I may need a lot more training, guys."

"Not as much as you think, baby." Nick kissed me, making my toes curl and my eyes well up. "Besides, we'll be making that decision, not you."

Trip placed his hands on my face, nudging me to look at him. He stared at me for the longest time. "Sweetheart, I can see in your eyes something is troubling you. I swear we won't put you on the center stage until you are ready. Okay?"

"Okay."

He pressed his lips to mine. I didn't feel like saying good-bye yet even though that was likely the best thing I could do.

I felt confused with their tenderness. It seemed like more than just training, but I wondered if I was just misreading everything. It was likely just another aspect of their teaching methods.

Damn, why couldn't things be different?

~

11:45 p.m.

BACK AT MY PLACE. Nick and Trip just left. They kissed me at the door. There was no going back now. I was in love with them.

I looked at my reflection in the mirror. "What's wrong with me?"

The entire day my two Dom trainers had pampered me. I didn't have to lift a finger for anything. They seemed to know what I wanted or needed before I even knew it myself. I enjoyed every second of it. They made me laugh, telling stories about their childhood. Though they were cousins, they were as close as brothers.

The more time I spent with them, the deeper and deeper I fell in love. They were funny, charming, and sincere.

When I filled them in on the details of losing my job, they were so sweet and supportive. They asked me what my plans were, and I told them I wasn't sure, though I did have an idea.

I'd never thought about starting my own business before, but after spending time with them, I was more excited than ever. My buried dreams of being in fashion had bubbled back up to the surface. I wanted to create a clothing line for people in the life, but I wasn't ready to share it with Nick and Trip. I didn't want them to think I was hoping to use their expertise in retail.

They took me to the club's munch after dinner at a local pub. I loved the low-pressure gathering. I learned so much and realized I wasn't the only newbie in the crowd.

After the munch, Nick and Trip took me back to the club for my third lesson.

I stripped off my clothes, recalling my time at The Cell this evening. We'd watched several demos. My education into the lifestyle was going well. The last session we observed was once again on the main stage. Three Doms had demonstrated various kinds of restraints on their naked sub—save for the collar around her neck—whose face revealed the complete trust she had for them.

On my bed, I started dreaming of what it would be like to be on that stage in front of all the members. But that would mean my lessons would be over, wouldn't it? That would be my graduation. That would mean my time with Nick and Trip would be over. I would be a fully trained sub but unattached to them or anyone.

I don't know how I would handle that, Diary. How could I go to the club and watch them with other subs? It would break my heart.

April 16th

11:01 p.m.

I am back at Nick and Trip's house. They are in the kitchen preparing a late-night snack for all of us. The time in their dungeon blew my mind. I feel like a smiling rag doll, completely relaxed and limp.

April 17th

I invited Nick and Trip to my place for dinner, which they were thrilled to accept. They were sitting in my living room while I finished up the last preparations for our meal.

"What is this, baby?" Nick asked.

I looked over the counter and saw he was holding up the sketchpad full of my designs for BDSM clothing. "Nothing," I lied. I still hadn't found the courage to tell him and Trip about my idea of starting my own line.

Both Nick and Trip turned to me, their faces stern. Clearly, they'd read through my hesitation.

"It's just some silly drawings of mine. Nothing important."

"Uh-huh." Nick opened the pad and showed the pages to Trip. "Very impressive, Misty."

"This is amazing, baby." Trip turned the pages.

As I stirred the sauce for our pasta, I kept glancing at the two Doms. Their smiles filled me with such pride. "Do you really like them?"

"Love them. You're incredibly talented." Nick turned to Trip. "Are you thinking what I'm thinking?"

Trip nodded.

"What are you talking about, guys?"

"We've been thinking about opening a clothing chain for people in the life," Nick said. "We believe there's a real need for this. Unlike here, lots of cities don't have one like Vivian's. We've talked to Vivian about this to get her input on how to make this work on a national level."

"I know she and Lex are good friends. Her store is amazing. Mia and Lea brought me a bunch of clothes from her shop."

"We're lucky to have her. In other cities, people have to order their outfits online, hoping they will fit. We want to have a safe place for people to try things on in every community."

"The plan is to duplicate Vivian's and open locations near all the top clubs around the country and world." Trip walked into the kitchen with my sketchpad. He opened it up to one of my favorite designs, meant for subs with curves like mine. "Your designs are beautiful, baby. Would you consider teaming up with us on this? We would love to feature your line in our stores. I'm betting Vivian would agree."

I was thrilled by their praise. "These are just the drawings, guys. Ideas. There's a ton of things that would have to be done to get these from the page and to the racks."

Nick came around the other side of me. "And guess what, baby? We have the connections to help with that. I think there's nothing that can stop the three of us if we work together. What do you say? Will you join me and Trip in this adventure?"

I kissed them both. "Yes. Yes. Yes."

I know this is only a business deal, Diary, but I can't help but hope it will turn into something more. I love them. I can't imagine living a single day without them in my life, graduation or not.

May 21st

I haven't been writing in this diary for some time. Too busy. The last several weeks have been a whirlwind of activity between my lessons and launching the business.

My kitchen table is littered with more drawings of mine. Nick and Trip have set up a fashion show for me this summer. Vivian has become president of the new retail chain, and she absolutely loves my designs. So much to do. Still, I can't seem to stop looking at the text Nick and Trip sent me about an hour ago. The last sentence had so much meaning.

Everything is about to change.

That was definitely putting it mildly. My whole life had been turned around because of them.

Nick and Trip had flown me to New York several times on their private jet for meetings. Yesterday, I'd given my final approval on my line. The examples the manufacturer presented us were exactly as I'd imagined them when I'd first conceived the idea.

A little over a week ago, the groundbreaking for *NTM Clothing and Toys* had been wonderful. People from around the world had attended, including the rich and famous, plus several movie stars and reality TV celebrities. I was on top of the world. I'd been shocked that Nick and Trip had made me an equal partner in the venture. At first, I'd tried to push back because I hadn't put any money in the business—only my designs. I told them none of us knew if my clothing line would be a success or not. They'd laughed, pointing to the reaction of the attendees to the mock-up drawings we'd brought to the groundbreaking.

Realizing they weren't going to give in to me, I signed the legal papers that made us partners. I was thrilled that the *M* in the name of the chain represented me.

I put away my sketchpad and read the text one more time.

Graduation Day, sweetheart. You're going to be up on center stage tomorrow night. We'll pick you up at 8 p.m. Everything is about to change.

When I first read the message I'd been so excited. I was a fully trained sub and had proven myself. Now, I was going to be welcomed into the community with open arms, but the only arms I cared to hold me were Nick's and Trip's. My joy of accomplishing so much so quickly subsided, realizing my lessons with them were coming to an end.

My heart is being ripped to shreds.

If I'm graduating, does that mean they will be moving on to another woman to train?

May 22nd

8:17 p.m.

I walked up onto the stage and got down on my knees in front of Nick and Trip. On the drive to the club, they'd told me that they were going to demonstrate the use of ropes in play.

Nick removed my clothing, leaving me completely naked.

Bondage was one of my favorite things in the lifestyle. Whenever they tied me up, I could feel my entire being surrender to them. They'd photographed me in various states of restraint and I found every picture beautiful.

My lips trembled as I wondered if this was my last time with Nick and Trip as my Doms. Regardless, I vowed to myself to make it the most memorable night of my life.

All my attention was on them. I was subtly aware of the crowd gathering for our show. What a change had occurred in me from that first demonstration they'd made me watch. The sub had been sent to a dreamy state by her Dom. Even though I'd imagined what it would be like to be up on this stage, I never thought it would be possible. But here I was. Nick and Trip had prepared me so well and had brought so much out of me. I felt whole for the first time in my life. I trusted them utterly, even if it broke my heart.

Trip cupped my chin, whispering so that only I could hear. "You okay, sweetheart?"

"Yes, Master. Yummy." *I'm going to reach that amazing dreamy state.*

He smiled and placed a blindfold over my eyes.

My Doms began tying me up with the ropes, informing the audience of all kinds of tips and tricks. I was vibrating like mad when they suspended me to the bar hanging from the ceiling. I couldn't move a muscle. I felt like I was floating, drifting above the stage like a feather. I could feel them spin me around so I was facing our audience now. I didn't feel any shame, only pride as the crowd began to applaud their approval.

I got so hot as they began caressing my body. They placed clamps on my nipples, causing me to get wet. I felt their tongues on my neck and I began to moan.

"We'd like to show you a little electric play." Nick's tone rumbled over my skin like a warm breeze. "Our sub responds beautifully to the violet wand."

Our sub? Hope sprang up inside me. Could it be true? Did they want me forever?

I felt the glass tube on my abdomen, delivering a sweet electric sting. My pussy began to ache and my clitoris began to throb.

They pressed the wand to various places on my body—my arms, my nipples, my thighs, my pussy. I was on fire. I began to writhe with desire in my restraints.

Fingers threaded through my swollen folds as lubrication was applied to my ass. Being on display added more fuel to the pressure building inside me. I grinned, realizing that I was not only a voyeur but an exhibitionist, also. I loved the way it made me feel.

I wondered if they were going to have sex with me in front of everyone. The thought excited me even more. Nick and Trip had released my inner vixen, crumbling the walls of doubt I'd lived with for so long. There was nothing wrong with pleasure, especially when you were with men you loved.

Keeping the blindfold on me, they untied me from the suspension bar.

"What state are you in, baby?" Nick asked.

"Yummy, Sir. So very yummy."

Trip removed the clamps.

Nick lifted me up off the ground, the blindfold still limiting my sight. I wrapped my arms and legs around him. He shoved his cock into my pussy, stretching me just right.

The crowd went wild, and I felt tears of joy well up in my eyes.

Trip whispered in my ear from behind. "Take a deep breath and let it out nice and slow."

Trembling, I answered, "Yes, Sir."

He sent his cock into my ass, pinning me even tighter between him and Nick. This was where I belonged. With them. Between them. Always.

Their strokes lengthened, going deeper into my pussy and ass. I trembled wildly as delicious dizziness spread out through me.

I came with a scream, uncaring who heard or what they thought. This was my time, my graduation, my ecstasy. They were my Doms. I couldn't hold back anything.

They stiffened, each slamming their cocks into my body with such force I thought I might actually pass out from the overwhelming passion.

I whimpered, feeling my lips trembling. I could hear the crowd jump to their feet with roaring applause.

With the blindfold still on, Nick and Trip dressed me and then carried me off stage. I wasn't sure why they wanted to keep me from seeing, but I trusted them completely. They were in charge. They knew what was best for me. Always.

I held onto Nick as tight as I could. I didn't want to let go.

I was aware they'd brought me to another room, one of the private ones. Was this good-bye? I would be completely lost without them, and I felt my heart starting to rip apart.

They lowered me down to a chair and took off the blindfold. As my eyes adjusted to the lighting of the room, I realized we were not alone.

Mia and Lex as well as Lea and her two Doms were standing only a few feet away from us.

I blinked several times. "Sirs?"

Nick and Trip each held one of my hands. In their other hands, they held together something that filled me with utter joy. *A collar.*

Nick smiled. "You are ours, baby. You changed our lives completely. I never thought I would settle down with anyone—*until you.*"

Trip nodded. "Won't you make us the happiest Doms on the planet and accept our collar, sweetheart?"

"Yummy. Yummy. Yummy. Yes. Of course, Masters."

"I love you, Misty." Nick kissed me.

"And I love you." Trip pressed his mouth to mine.

As we continued kissing, I knew my future was only beginning.

The End

READ on for an excerpt from The Marine in Unit A, book 1 of Lee Swift's gay romance / new adult series Mockingbird Place...

Excerpt

The Marine in Unit A
Book 1 of Mockingbird Place

The man who has been more of a dad to me than my biological father is dead.

He rescued me from the streets six years ago—a runaway teenage boy, escaping a family who thought I was an abomination.

Now what do I do? I have no one.

My life might look great from the outside. I'm in college. I have my own apartment. I have lots of friends.

But I'm dying on the inside.

I feel so alone. Lost. Hopeless.

I'm not the kind of person to wallow in self-pity. I need a distraction.

The guy moving into Unit A may be just what I need to take my mind off of losing my dad.

21-year old Oliver Lancaster is attracted to 22-year old Adam Stockton, the former-Marine moving into Unit A. But attraction for the closeted man morphs quickly into something deeper, something meaningful, something that terrifies Oliver. What will happen if Adam learns about the secret from his past?

Warning: contains skinny dipping, two hot men kissing, and sexual situations taking place in a 10-unit Mediterranean complex filled with college-aged hotties.

~

EXCERPT:

I walk to my car and spot Adam alone trying to wrestle a chair out of a U-Haul truck with an empty tow dolly. A white Honda Pilot filled with clothes and sporting California plates is parked next to the truck. "Nice ride, Adam. You look like you could use some help. Where's your friend?"

"He didn't show." Adam shrugs. "Called in sick, so to speak." A smile appears on his handsome face. The earlier tension I sensed from him is gone. "I have to get this truck back by eight in the morning or pay for another day."

"So much for this umbrella." I fold it up and set it to the side.

"Aren't you meeting your friends?"

"I was." I remember how uptight he became when I mentioned the strip club. *I'm not gay, Oliver.* I bring out my cell. "I'll send them a text. They'll understand."

"Oliver, I can find someone else."

"Why bother since I'm here?" I send the text and put my phone away. "Let's get busy."

I roll up my sleeves and help him carry the chair to Unit A. We walk inside.

Adam and I put the chair down next to the front door.

It is so strange seeing the apartment without Malcolm's things. The only items inside are a few of Adam's boxes.

It seems like Malcolm is whispering to me that Unit A is no longer his, that it now belongs to Adam. I'm going to have to get used to calling this Adam's place. I'm not sure I will ever feel comfortable about that.

"Very different from when I lived here."

"You lived in this apartment? With the guy who died?"

"I did. Malcolm Rivers owned Mockingbird Place. He gave me my start here in Dallas." I can feel my grief creeping back in.

"Were you...I mean..."

"No. We weren't a couple, if that's what you were asking. He was like a father to me. And even though he was in his eighties, he was a blast to be around. The last party we had here was his eighty-second birthday. That was just a month ago, and only three weeks before he... before he..." I can't bring myself to say *before he died*. "Three weeks before Malcolm's heart attack."

Adam put his hand on my shoulder. "We don't have to talk about this now if it's too hard on you."

I look into his kind eyes and shake my head. "No. It's fine. Actually talking about him helps. We had so much fun celebrating his birthday. What a great party, though it wound down before ten. Unusual for Malcolm. A sign of what was to come with him that I should have noticed but didn't."

"I'm sorry you've gone through all this, Oliver. I really can do this by myself. It's got to be hard on you seeing me move into your friend's apartment, much less helping me do it."

His words melt my heart. Adam is one of the good guys.

"No. I want to help. Malcolm would want me to move on."

"Clearly a very wise man. Do you have a photo of him?"

I pull out my phone and bring up the pic of Malcolm and me standing next to his birthday cake.

"I like his smile and yours," Adam says.

"Malcolm told us he was tired and since we were all so young, we should go out to the clubs without him. He said it would be the best present any of us could give him. I stayed behind and helped him clean up. I had a strange feeling that something was wrong with him. But in typical Malcolm-fashion, after the last dish was put away, he insisted I go join everyone else. 'You're twenty-one, Oliver, not eighty-two. Go have fun.' God, I wonder if he knew what was coming."

"Whether he did or didn't, Malcolm obviously cared about you."

"Yes, he did. If I'd known I was going to lose Malcolm so soon, I would have refused to leave him. More than that even. I would have insisted on moving back into my old room here. It might have changed the outcome, even though the doctors told us there was nothing that could have saved him."

"Maybe this is hard to accept right now, and maybe I don't even have the right to say it—but what you've already told me about Malcolm, I believe he would not want you to beat yourself up with what-ifs. He would want you to be happy and think about the time you had together."

I look at Adam—really look at him. There is something very special about him. "You may not have known Malcolm but you're absolutely right. When I moved out almost a year ago I knew he was sad, though he never admitted it to me. In fact, Malcolm told *me* not to be sad. I put my arm around him and reminded him that we would only be a few doors away from each other. His eyes welled up. Then Malcolm told me we needed to remember what good times we had living together but not to dwell on the past."

"Why did you move into Unit F?" Adam asks.

"Malcolm thought I should have my own space. Told me I needed to spread my wings. I wasn't so sure. I liked living with him."

"He sounds like he was a terrific guy."

"He *was*." That word still makes me cringe when referring to Malcolm. Will I ever get used to it? I doubt it. "Even though I know he would have preferred for me to continue living with him, he never let on. That's the kind of man Malcolm Rivers was, always thinking of others and their needs."

"I wish I could have known him."

I smile. Why is it so easy for me to talk to Adam? "You would have liked him, and I know he would have liked you." I try to shake off the sadness so that we can get back to work. "Where do you want the chair?"

"I don't know. Where do you think it should go?"

"That corner by the window looks best right now, but a final decision can be made once the rest of your stuff is inside."

We are only able to get a few more of Adam's things into the apartment before the rain starts coming down hard.

"We better take a break until this slows down some." Adam reaches into a box marked *Bathroom* and pulls out a couple of towels.

I sit down on the wooden floor that once held Malcolm's large Persian rug.

Adam tosses a towel to me and begins drying off with another towel himself.

It's so nice to see him relax. Could I be wrong about him being gay? Maybe he isn't closeted. But something in my gut tells me otherwise.

"I've got wine but I haven't unpacked the glasses. I think they're still on the truck. There is beer in the fridge I bought for my buddy and me. Would you like one?"

I nod, noticing once again his slight limp as he walks to his refrigerator. "Sarah told me you're an ex-Marine."

"There are no *ex*-Marines, Oliver." He returns to the living room with two beers, sits down next to me on the floor, and hands me one. "There are two ways that inactive Marines are referred to. Me? I'm *former* Marine, since I didn't reach retirement. Far from it. I'm only twenty-two." He grins, making him appear even sexier than before, though I think that's impossible. "For those who did serve twenty-plus, we call them *retired* Marines."

"I've heard the saying 'Once a Marine, always a Marine.'"

"That's right. I bleed Marine green like my brothers and sisters." He holds up his beer. "Thanks for helping. I really appreciate it."

"My pleasure. Welcome to the neighborhood."

End of Excerpt

Also by Lee Swift

Novels

Morvicti Blood *(Supernatural Thriller)*

Cupid's Arrow *(Gay Fantasy Romance)*

Three to Play *(Menage MMF Romance)*

(All series listed in best reading order)

Mockingbird Place

(Gay Romance Series)

The Marine in Unit A

The Cowboy in Unit E

The Fireman in Unit C

The Doctor in Unit H

The Fighter in Unit J

Holiday Beaus (Novella)

The Musician in Unit G

The Cop in Unit B

Wolf Pack

(Menage MFM Romance Trilogy)

Secret Cravings

Primal Desires

Delicious Hunger

Eternal Trio Series

(Gay Menage Fantasy Romance)

Levi's Rogues

Perfection

Secret Diary Series

(Erotic Straight BDSM Trilogy)

Mia's Spanking Diary

Misty's Bondage Diary

Lea's Ménage Diary

Writing with Lana Lynn

(Thrillers)

Lexi's Protector *(Men Without A Cause)*

Liz's Guardian *(Men Without A Cause)*

About the Author

Lee Swift, who writes under several pen names including Kris Cook, creates novels, short stories, screenplays and more.

With an unquenchable thirst to experience all his life journey has to offer, Lee and hubby love travel but still call Dallas, Texas home.

Signup for Lee's Newsletter.